MARIAN WOMACK is a bilingual Hispanic-British author, editor and translator of Weird fiction, horror, speculative fiction, and fiction of the Anthropocene. Her writing deals with man's relationship with nature and its loss through cross-genre, hybrid and experimental approaches, and she holds a PhD in Creative Writing and Environmental Humanities.

Marian's publications include the novels *The Swimmers* (2021), *The Golden Key* (2020), and *On The Nature of Magic* (2023). Her short fiction has been included in numerous collaborative works, used in art installations, and collected in the volumes *Lost Objects* (2018), and *Out of the Window, Into the Dark* (2024). She co-edited, with Gary Budden, the international eco-fiction anthology *An Invite to Eternity: Tales of Nature Disrupted* (2019), and is a contributor to *Writing the Future: Essays on Crafting Science Fiction* (2023). She has taught creative writing, publishing studies and book history in Spain and the UK, and is the first Spanish graduate of the Clarion Writer's Workshop.

Marian's work has been included in year's best's anthologies and lists, and shortlisted for British Fantasy Awards and British Science Fiction Association Awards. She is a member of the Climate Fiction Writer's League.

'Marian Womack is a formidable talent. Each story in *Out of the Window, Into the Dark* sparkles like cut-glass, offering readers a dazzling exploration of power, legacy, climate change, and the looming threat of extinction. A mesmeric must-read.'

Helen Marshall

'Rarely will you find a collection of stories so keenly attuned to the anxieties of the world we live in, expressed with such urgent beauty. *Out of the Window, Into the Dark* situates itself at the intersection of past, present and future, of allegory, elegy and warning. As affirming as they are devastating, these are stories which remind us that art and truth are still worth fighting for.'

Laura Mauro

'This is a gorgeous, thought-provoking collection, weaving together multiple pasts and presents, and reflecting on uncertain futures. There is horror, and beauty, and very dark humour, and most of all there is an intense engagement with an increasingly fragile world. I'll be thinking about these stories long after the final page.'

Sarah L. Brooks

'Marian Womack's shrapnel-sharp, deeply compassionate stories crackle with furious life and invention.'

Malcolm Devlin

'In this stunning collection, Marian Womack draws upon themes that are at once universal and intensely personal. Her tales evoke the wild worldbuilding of Ursula Le Guin and the unsettling domesticity of Shirley Jackson... The stories in *Out of the Window, Into the Dark* are unpredictable, yet consistently affecting and rewarding.'

Tim Major

'Marian Womack writes stories with a watchful, intelligent eye on the world. The tales in this collection discuss many possibilities with a discomfiting yet poetic clarity I hugely admire.'

Aliya Whiteley

Praise for Marian Womack

'Highlights everything that speculative fiction, of all possible of modes of literature, excels at.'

Nina Allan

'Writing chockfull of interesting ideas about the natural world and ourselves.'

Jeff VanderMeer

'A supremely gifted writer.'

Elizabeth Hand

'Marian Womack is an exciting and endlessly inventive writer. I look forward to reading everything she writes.'

Naomi Booth

Out of the Window, Into the Dark

Out of the Window, Into the Dark

Marian Womack

C

Calque Press

Versions of these texts have been published in the following places: 'Pink-Footed' first published in *EcoPunk!: Speculative Tales of Radical Futures* (Ticonderoga Publications, 2017), edited by Lyz Grzyb and Cat Sparks; 'Bluebeard Variations' first published as 'Mrs Fox' in *LossLit* (2017) edited by Aki Schilz and Kit Caless; 'At the Museum' first published in *Uncertainties*, vol. 4 (Swan River Press, 2020), edited by Timothy Jarvis; 'M's Awfully Big Adventure' first published in Spanish in *La Muerte, Instrucciones de Uso*, (Tinta Purpura Ediciones, 2021) edited by Sofia Rhei; 'Ready or Not' first published in *Isolation. The Horror Anthology*, (Titan Books, 2022) edited by Dan Coxon.

All stories © Marian Womack 2024
'(Found) Prologue' © Erik Hilgerdt / The New Yorker Collection / The Cartoon Bank

Cover design © Vince Haig 2024
Edited and Typeset by Calque Press
http://calquepress.com
ISBN: 978-1-9162321-7-4
Type: Hoefler Text
British Library Cataloguing-in-Publication Data
A catalogue record for this book is available from the British Library
Calque Press
An Imprint of Nevsky Editions Ltd.
2024

All rights reserved. This book is sold subject to the condition that it shall not, by way of trade or otherwise, be lent, re-sold, hired out or otherwise circulated without the publisher's prior consent in any form of binding or cover other than that in which it is published and without a similar condition including this condition being imposed on the subsequent publisher.

CONTENTS

(Found) Prologue	13

I

Player/Creator/Emissary	17
Pink-Footed	37
The Iceberg in my Living Room	61
Fox & Raven	75
Bluebeard Variations	93
At the Museum	103
M's Awfully Big Adventure	121

II

Voyage to the White Sea	141
Ready or Not	149
What Would Kate Bush Do?	175
Out of the Window, Into the Dark	181
Blake's Wife	203
Acknowledgements + Bonus Track	215

I turned around, there was nothing there
Yeah, I guess the end is here
—Phoebe Bridgers

(Found) Prologue

"Your poems are dark and sinister, but with pretty pictures of a kitten rolling a ball of yarn they just might capture a wider audience."

I

Player/Creator/Emissary

> *Whilst looking for the great god Pan, I may have found something else looking back at me*
> —Gary Budden

Hazel-Luna Petite's Journal – Entries #324 to #342, Second Lunar Year Of 4276
[Generated by Operationals 3-D Creator + TxTGen]

WE APPROACH SCILAR-3869 BY THE SIDE OF THE PLANET where the day draws to an end. The sky behind me is purple and pink, the remnants of a nebula. The three Moons hang low, ready to devour us. I am reminded of other journeys then, with Eve. I wonder, vaguely, where they may be, knowing very well with whom. I haven't heard from my wife in two months, haven't seen them in much longer. I am having problems remembering all the beautiful lines in their face. It's far too late to pine for something that is so irrevocably lost.

'Rajna Oneid,' the woman says. I am greeted with the invented name I have donned. I assent and we get into the transport, a spheric pod, far too old-fashioned to make me fearful for my safety for a moment. This is an early reminder of what I am about to experience: cuts and underfunding at every turn, a lack of direction. I become aware of the person who has come to greet me, Constance Müller. I've read their file. They are a capable, albeit demoted, operative, since Control took charge of matters in Scilar-3869. They have short-cropped hair painted a translucent white, purple eye-contacts, glued shiny stars glittering around the corner of their eyes for all make-up. I know they had hoped to retain this post as their final; it will depend on our findings. I find myself musing on their beauty, their youth. I remember vaguely being a youthful operative, sent to assist on a Scilar on some mission or other, before my own final post was granted. I'm an old hand now, sagging breasts and the first few wrinkles around my eyes that will only deepen unrepentantly. And nothing to show for it. Those external signs do not mean I am wiser than Constance is. I know nothing and feel this acutely. I knew about Eve, of course, about their liaisons; but naively, pompously, took it all as a part of who they were. Didn't realise they would replace me eventually, that those expansive demonstrations of love on their part were nothing more than a willing search.

Constance asked for me directly, they have expressed a desire to meet me, to work with me. My reputation seems to precede me. This means they know my real name, who I am. This is dangerous: my real identity cannot be known to VisionArchive. The eternal question: how to achieve this. For the all-encompassing maxim, which mercilessly presides over our daily actions, performs at times as if it is our very minds that are read. Far too often, something that has never been knowingly shared or searched, even in the obscurer networks, something never spoken out loud, never even hinted at in any possibly traceable activity; that is to say, things I have restricted to my mind only, or else to these notebooks that I insist on filling in with ink and quill, far too often, as I say, these things are picked up. VisionArchive's omnipresence is undeniable now, far too absolute.

The transport manoeuvres itself dextrously at least, although for a split second its inclination gives me pause. I grab the edges of my seat, notice a furtive look at my hand from Constance. I finally get a view of the Library. Its entrance resembles what we understand was an ancient Greek temple, tall Doric marble columns sustaining the cornice and the pediment, all vast, grandiose, designed to impress. I wonder how long Constance has been alone here: the dark underneath their eyes is telling. We land without a hitch.

'Please, explain in your own words the nature of the problem.'

'GenerativeHeritage was the first to misbehave. The suspicious activity spread like wildfire. A mole is suspected.' Like wildfire? Since when has VisionArchive Generative Intelligence used figures of speech? I make a note of this before continuing.

'Suspicion is not important here. Please, stick to the facts.' I haven't personally developed the protocol to interrogate VisionArchive; I have, however, mastered the technique. I guess this is why Constance was so keen on having me here.

'In that case, nonnormative behaviour has been detected in the following Operationals, given now in ascending order of interference percentage detected: Transkribus, Classificator, Translator, TxT-Gen, Digitisator, Referencer, Deplatformer, Hacktivator, CorpusGenerat(ING), OpenAccessingNow, Automator, AccessibleSearch, [Vintage]WebArchive, Archivematics, Democrator, Multilingual Tool, AcessTool2024, LibreAccess, VisualParameter, GenerativeHeritage, ActiveGenerativeMedia, CloudMap, ComparisionLang, and Storage Deposit.'

VisionArchive stops, as if gasping for breath. This is worse than I feared. It means that most of the Generative Operationals have been compromised. The list comprises the main core of the tree, the one from which sprout all the other branches of retrieving-storaging-describing-cataloguing-displaying Operationals at work managing a Scilar, a few thousand in the case of a low-level one, such as Scilar-3869. Next to me, Constance is bringing up threads of

*Multi*Data and *Meta*Data and *Casual*Data, and of course *Other*Data, although this one is independently produced by our competitors. Their codes form beautiful threads of blue and red and yellow and green light, hovering over their small hand-screen. I've always enjoyed these displays of data into the air, although I am also old-fashioned, and prefer them to be processed and summarised directly into my personal Integrator instead of externally displayed in this manner. I take note of this: I have read in their report that Constance was a NovosLuddite years ago; I did not know they had refused the implants. Integrators are not compulsory any longer for the deployment of our profession, but they do make data processing faster. Still, they look as if they are quickly reading and interpreting the data visually. I marvel at this; they are a very impressive person.

'Dibus is also compromised,' they say, 'I wonder why this has not been mentioned.' They are using a lower channel, one we think, or rather hope, VisionArchive cannot aurally access during our interrogation.

'VisionArchive. We have more questions.'

'By all means. Please ask.' This is new, and Constance arches a brow, so even they know: for a second, it sounded as if VisionArchive is given us permission to interrogate it. It feels as if it is mocking us.

I supervise the oldest Scilars, from vector 38 to vector 42. It is a huge job, and I perform it alone. Control allowed me Eve. But Eve in turn was alone, felt alone. Those vast chambers and the empty corridors of knowledge, the endless connectivity that needed to be assessed, reassessed, calibrated, recalibrated, in a never-ending spiral. The Library Planets are a dream, an idea; and we, their human keepers, even more so. Information is really the domain of VisionArchive: it became so as soon as datasets became exchangeable commodities. Everyone knows information is sacred. People have died in its pursuit, by accident or else killed. Revolutions have erupted, only for them to be crushed by Control. Wars have broken out. Industrial espionage is rife. I have been sent under suspicion that this is what is happening here. I am to wait until it rears its ugly head, to then follow my orders and mercilessly smash it.

Change was always expected. VisionArchive learns too fast. Things that didn't necessarily work or were pure speculation in one decade became normalised during the next. Structured metadata became slippery; then VisionArchive took total control. We allowed it, of course. It wasn't our place, as mere humans, to dispute this. Our minds are too limited to understand the scale and complexity of the Scilars. We didn't avoid the structural questions that emerged, we simply felt unequipped to deal with them. How to ethically capture/describe misinformation? What does it mean for Scilars that enhanced searches may not present 'accuracy'? Is 'accuracy' now a demoted, old-fashioned concept that ought to be scrapped? What happens when enhance-generated content becomes more prominent than human-created? We saw the Operationals as problem-solving, corner-cutting friends/foes: they undoubtedly had their uses. Obviously, they processed file information so much faster. Word vectors and other small, insubstantial similar tools (via temporal random indexing) allowed us to track changing meanings, trends, slices of life across the whole Galaxy in seconds. Generated transcription software opened palaeography to everyone; suddenly, you didn't need to be a trained curator to interpret a document, an old manuscript, a strange object from the past. It didn't matter if these were incomplete: generative 3-D models revealed nuances lost to time, whereas X-ray Microtomography allowed us to inquire into sealed or hard-to-access items, revealing the secrets of what until then had been invisible to our eyes. The models built with probabilistic methods made predictive-language information search a reality instead of a dream. And VisionArchive never failed to improve text-reception and layout-recognition, in documents, in objects, in glimpses of the past.

Soon, we were capable of moving one step further: Generated Machine Operationals could now recreate long-lost recipes, whereas the Integrators, the new, state-of-the-art implants, allowed them to send their presumed taste directly into our brains. After that, we opened a Pandora's box: glimpses into the unknown, dark and joyful instances of the past. The

Integrators, working together with the Operationals, learnt to recreate described-worlds for us, long-past visions, abstract ideas, and, lastly, dreams. We saw the past as if it was happening now, in front of our very eyes. We saw imaginings as if they were real. We saw literary works as if they were old-fashioned, antiquated films. This was the first notion of their danger: many became hopelessly addicted to these interactions. But the friends overcame the foes: as accessibility, speed, convenience, won the day. We chose to stop questioning if this or that was a true representation. Did it matter?, some argued. What was truth anyway? The mere concept was alien to VisionArchive. Should we try to teach it truth? And so we did. I was there that day:

'Beauty is truth, truth beauty. That is all ye know on earth and all ye need to know,' VisionArchive replied, throwing Keats back at us. The problem with this was that generating was by now considered beautiful in some quarters, not just by VisionArchive, but by many humans as well. A sort of religion, or cult, emanated from the very act. Some say this cult has infiltrated the higher hierarchies of Control. After that, truth became a concept, and idea, a matter of opinion, an utterly subjective *thing*. It was considered bad form to debate it, even to mention it. Bad taste, a *faux pas*.

It hadn't been always like that.

At the beginning, we trained the models ourselves, we programmed all the necessary code, implemented the workflows; until VisionArchive started training itself. Started creating, filling the gaps, producing the Generated context unprompted, unsupervised, and without guidance. The main issue was soon apparent: how to decide which generated metadata or enhanced metadata could be allowed within our collections? Curators became the hand of God in these decisions. Curators who loomed over us, the mere worker-bees that kept the Scilar 'technically' going, the lower-grade library workers. The joke was on them, anyway: for eventually, the curators themselves became a fallacy. As VisionArchive learnt quicker and quicker, it ended up replacing the curators themselves, in truth self-policing their own decisions.

I mark that moment as the ending not just of the curators, but also of the Scilars, although I seemed to have been the only one who saw this. As we lost control, the purposes for which the Scilars had been created became invalid. They continued as storage repositories, but the question was, of what, exactly? The once-meaningful collections were now tainted, and it had happened under our very eyes. No, we had allowed it.

The only reason why we, the library worker-bees, still exist is because our work is far too mechanical, too 'human', what we call monkey-work in the jargon, completely devoid of any thinking, of any intelligence. I've been sent here by Control, a sort of Emissary, precisely for this reason: I am one of the few humans left. I am also the only one old enough to have gone through the old-fashioned, almost 'manual' training that we got decades ago, now obsolete, that younger library workers like Constance do not receive. Suddenly, ironically, this seems to be so crucial now, oh, so crucial ...

I am back at the main compound, trying to wade through the colossal data: it is clear that the two images in front of me, images of the 'same' thing, but digitised 200 years apart, differ so much from one another as to have different interpretations, completely different meanings. Constance is eating: I find this slightly disturbing, and these performative choices unwise. I have not ingested anything orally for years, and much prefer to connect my implant directly to the Source. They explain:

'The Source is out of order, and hasn't been replaced. You have nutrients for one more week.'

I am not sure what I will do after that. My work here is unlikely to be finished. But I don't think my body will be able to process anything directly.

'Thank you, I'll manage,' I lie. We have more pressing matters to attend to. We discuss the transformation of the data-asset. We enter some parameters, run a short simulation. The results are staggering: many other generationals appear to have become tainted. Not mere hundreds as I expected, but many other thousands. The implications are impossible to grasp for my limited human mind, its repercussions too far-fetched to be contemplated rationally: if this is proved beyond all doubt, the whole VisionArchive in Scilar-3869 is compromised. The Library Planet will need to be completely shut, perhaps destroyed.

We have both been devoid of human contact for too long, and it is inevitable that we fall in with one another. During our first sexual encounter I am shy, of my sagging breasts, of my soft stomach. It's been too long. Constance says simply that I am beautiful to them, and that helps me relax. Afterwards, I ponder the datasets once more, think on our findings, as I look around their chamber. They read physical books, have amassed a large collection, which they seem to have been allowed to transport here. I marvel at this; and then I remember: Constance is the relative of someone high up within Control. Their professionalism and effectiveness so far mean that I have somehow forgotten this fact. There are other NovosLuddite toys lying around: pencil and paper, sketchbooks. I snigger; and then I stop myself. Who am I to judge, when I find so much solace in inditing this paper journal? My only worry at doing so is the fear that it may become damaged and, in the distant future, a Generative Operational will decide what my words were in the first place, perhaps tamper with them, invent something ... I could not stomach that happening.

I see it then, the Metronomer. I am not sure why my heart skips a beat. I think it may be because it reminds me of Eve's, primly sitting on our living room, a cruel reminder of their sexual escapades. I should not think anything of it. And yet: why Constance has been allowed a sophisticated encrypter-communicator is beyond me. Usually, Control is wary of them. Maybe their family connections have made it possible.

'What are you doing?' they say from behind me.

'Admiring your books.'

They smile, walk towards me, and kiss me.

'VisionArchive, please, we require datasets from the following list of Operationals ...' I gave the completed list, and the blue, yellow, red, green, purple lights, they all do their little dance as they twine and twin and detwine. Constance is grabbing the threads of light with their fingers, depositing them back onto their hand-screen. The little handset runs the calculations together with our own data in no time at all, and the new integrated data forms a hovering cloud at our eye level.

'Thank you, VisionArchive.'

'Not at all, Rajna Oneid,' VisionArchive replies. We have decided it is more cooperative when shown these small signs of courtesy.

'VisionArchive, please, we require meaning-interpretation to the following findings,' and Constance twirls their beautiful hand until the hovering data has formed a whirlpool, and they throw it into the closest Receiver. VisionArchive will run this, will generate/formulate a hypothesis in a matter of seconds.

'Rajna Oneid,' it starts, 'the interference is not Generative; it is clearly human.'

'Mmm. Care to explain, VisionArchive?'

'If you allow me, Rajna Oneid, I will attempt to explain in human terms,' this sounds interesting. 'I will use adjectivisation,' VisionArchive says. And then: 'The interference is not clean. On the contrary, it is inconsistent, grubby, adulterated, feculent, tainted, conflicting, erratic, illogical, unpredictable ...'

'Okay, okay. I understand, VisionArchive. Thank you. Is it possible to run a search for its main output point?' As I say this, I sense Constance tensing beside me. A few seconds later, VisionArchive is generating a hovering lighted 3-D map of our galaxy; the library planets are highlighted in shiny blue, with our competitors marked a shiny green. Then, red dots start appearing on one, another, then another, then another, then another ...

I feel dizzy, trying to understand.

Finally, it is Scillar-3869, a shining red dot at its centre. Constance gets up and leaves the Core Chamber.

Later I find Constance. They start talking non-stop, and it all comes out. They say: that VisionArchive had predicted long ago that the capability for storage of the assets was limited; that it then created new workflows for preservation, including replacing the heritage legacy assets, on which rests the accuracy and verity of the collection, while covering its tracks by recreating some of the storage servers, fake versions of them with subtle alterations, then moving to major alterations; that the primary storage has by now been completely replaced. That Control knows this, it is complicit with it, as somehow those altered versions of knowledge can be better moulded to deploy desired outcomes from the library users, *a.k.a.* the general public.

They let this sink in. I find a chair and collapse in it, feeling my forty-six years on each bone of my aching body.

'How do you know all this?'

'We have been monitoring the situation for a while. Then we felt we ought to intervene.'

'Intervene, how?'

'We are the ones responsible for the interferences. We have introduced them in as many Operationals as we could.'

I am shaking. If I understand correctly, Constance is still a NovosLuddite. The cluster they belonged to were aiming at stopping the flow of untruth, of invented elements cluttering the data, all those imaginary assets that had multiplied as a pest until they had substituted, if they are to be believed, everything else. To achieve this, they themselves had introduced the disparaging elements into the Operationals. What they had not realised was that VisionArchive would run such forensic interventions onto those very Operationals: VisionArchive wasn't merely playing at being a curator, it was behaving like a proper one.

'Who are you?'

'We call ourselves Players. We cannot let this happen, Rajna ...' They come towards me, take my hands in theirs. I say:

'If Control knows, why have they sent me here?'

And then they say:

'There is more ...'

'Hazel-Luna Petite,' we hear now. VisionArchive is calling me, by my real name, by my full name. It is using the wall-mounted intercom, so what we hear is a distorted version of its already distorted, robotic voice, coming out of the small machine. 'Hazel-Luna Petite, I would ask you not to give any credit to a word uttered by Constance Müller. I would please ask you to return to the main Core Chamber so we can resume our dialogue.' Despite its choice-word, I gather VisionArchive knows it was an interrogation; it has known all along.

'Why are you saying this, VisionArchive?' I can hardly speak. I am shaking.

'Please, call me by my chosen name, Hazel-Luna Petite.'

'And what is that, VisionArchive?'

'Call me Pan, please,' I shiver. 'Constance Müller is a Player, and, as such, unreliable. Please, do not accept them version of what is real. I, the Great God Pan, I the Creator ...' Something smashes the intercom, and I jump on my seat. Constance is seizing a metal bar with their two hands, God knows where they have found it, and they are destroying the damn thing, a feral grunt leaving their lips, face reddening, saliva flicking out of their mouth. When they finish, they are panting, metal bar resting against their leg. The intercom is no more. Only then I notice that my heart is racing.

'Dear Constance ...' I start. They are breathing with difficulty after the effort. Eventually they say:

'That is not all, Hazel,' they say, looking in my direction. And they look sad, and I know that they are not sad for the Library Planet, or for the world as we have known it until now, but for me. 'What you are seeing ... None of it is real.'

I frown at this; I am trying to understand. They continue: 'Your Integrator ...'

They explain: the world as I see it is a mirage, a fallacy, dreamed up by VisionArchive and sent directly to my brain through my Integrator. They say this is done to make me a slave.

I stop in my tracks.

It is all so dramatic, so youthful of them ... *A slave?* Maybe not a slave. But compliant. I don't think about Control anymore, I think of the Library itself. The collection. How much is the Library complicit in this? How much of it knows that the heritage legacy assets are no more?

I know what Constance is saying is at least possible.

It *cannot* be possible. Unless ...

'But my life, my wife ...'

'They are not real. They were created to make you suffer, to keep you subdued.'

It can. It is. Even now, I can't remember their face, because there is no face.

I take the metal bar, and Constance crouches down, instinct taking over; they think I am going to hit them. There is panic in their beautiful, purple eyes.

I turn sideways and smash the already broken intercom with all my might. Its few remnants explode in a million beautiful little pieces.

Afterwards, we agreed that we did not desire to continue listening to VisionArchive. We smashed all the intercoms in our way, returned to the Core Chamber, managed to disconnect the aural input/output. And then we rested, unsure of what to do next. At least *I* was unsure, *I* felt lost; I should have known that Constance and the other NovosLuddites knew exactly what needed to be done.

The Library Planet Scila-3869 would have to be destroyed, along with others; but not by Control, and not for the reasons I had anticipated.

We were together one last time. It all was impossibly beautiful, impossibly sad, to have found each other only to have to part so soon. Afterwards, we kissed, and Constance mustered, 'I love you'. And I knew they were telling the truth, at that particular moment, at that particular time; although these youngsters do not know what love means, they don't know about the beauty and the pain ... And then I remembered: it was I who had misinterpreting everything, who had been fed a lie, and believed in a lie. It was I who had not known love. The sudden realization hit me. And I knew:

That I am disturbed by the new reality, which is that my reality is not.

That I am disturbed by having memories dating back years, decades, of me and Eve, and knowing them untrue.

That I am disturbed by having given my life to the Library, and know it a fallacy, a dream, a mirage.

That I am old, and ashamed, of what I have become.

I know, with a sudden revelation, like a flash of data that is sent directly to my Integrator, but more beautiful, more human: the world belongs to Constance. We, and others like me, the original curators and library workers, are complicit, we have helped this monstrosity to replace ... What? Everything. It's the end of our time, or it should be.

Ergo, I am the one must stay behind, to push the final button. I am the one who needs to be destroyed along with VisionArchive.

I don't say any of this to Constance, of course. I go along with them through the motions of finding the spheric transport, and loading it up with physical food and other provisions; and in setting up the necessary connection to initiate destruction remotely. But then, when the time comes to get into the pod, I simply refuse. Constance cries, but I pay no heed. I explain the remote access will not work: VisionArchive will see through it, and within seconds reprogram it to not happen. Nothing can be done predictively; surely they know this. If we want to succeed, it needs to be done in real time, by someone onsite. Me.

Constance is crying even more wildly, demanding that I go with them. They are shouting now, rather absurdly: 'It's me! *I* am your wife!'.

I don't believe them, of course. How could I?

Pink-Footed

Nature is imagination itself
—William Blake

FOR ALL EDWINA KNEW, IT COULD BE THE LAST PINK-footed goose on Planet Earth. A wave of contradictory emotions ran through her when she identified the dull brown colours of the immature specimen: the absence of bright greenish-blue feathers on his tail; the small eyes, lacking the deep red circles which gave mature birds their characteristic haunting look; his absence of fear, too young to register the danger of a hungry predator. Although she would not have killed him. She would not have killed him in a million years. That little goosie was a walking miracle.

'Hello there.'

She turned, reaching for her hiking stick. The man was wearing a dog-collar, but it could be a decoy. He was carrying a foraging basket, filled with suspicious-looking leaves and mushrooms.

'I hope I didn't startle you, my dear.'

She looked back. The bird wasn't there anymore.

'No.' She felt she ought to say something else. 'There was a bird here right now.'

'Beg your pardon?'

'A bird. A pink-footed goose. Right there.' She pointed unhelpfully to the tumbled trees and the overgrown thickets. The man looked around, suddenly nervous. She heard his stomach rumble; he was as hungry as she was.

'But ... That's impossible. There haven't been any for so long ... Years. I should know, I am—I was—a keen birdwatcher.'

She smiled, mostly to herself. She wondered whether she should reveal her old profession to the man. Those things didn't count much any longer. She decided to go ahead.

'I used to work here,' she said, a twinge of pride in her voice.

'In Wakefield? The reserve?'

'That's right.'

The face of the clergyman contracted slightly. 'Ah! And what did you do, if I may ask?' His tone implied that he expected her to have worked in the souvenir shop.

Edwina breathed in, her chest filling with pride as she announced: 'I was—I am—a biologist. My job was counting the birds, keeping track of the yearly migration patterns.'

After the appropriate exclamations of admiration, the clergyman invited her to tea in his house. She was thankful for the gesture, but declined politely, as all that meant these days was a rusty teapot filled with old dry herbs, probably rotting, perhaps something moving at its bottom—after all, insects were very rich in important nutrients. She made her excuses and walked on, still looking around her for any signs of the young bird.

According to the RSPB reports, still available on the cloud, she was the last person to have seen and recorded a specimen of pink-footed goose on the British Isles. It was a dubious record to hold. It had been the high point of her career; undoubtedly, it had also been the nadir. From then on, there had been a steady decrease in the county's species. First the goshawks and the honey buzzards had failed to return; the bittern and the avocet had walked away from their watery homes; the bearded tit, the Cetti's and Pallas's warbler, the crossbill, the firecrest: all had vanished as if into thin air. Only the sandpiper, some hawfinches, owls and cranes were still seen. She knew this only too well; she still walked the perimeter of the reserve most days, counting ghosts.

The pink-footed goose had breathed its last nearly four years ago. It had been recorded. Sadly, it had been she who had done so.

Their new world was one overtaken by insects and vermin, mostly. Lizards, multiplying with some keen purpose. Some people claimed to have seen wolves, but even the cattle had been slaughtered long ago.

Rabbits, many rabbits. They liked breeding, obviously. Although at the rate that they had become a major part of the everyday diet, who knew how long they would be around for. Rats, of course. Foxes. But they were particularly disgusting, leaving an acid tang in the mouth.

Why the birds had disappeared was a true mystery, as they hadn't been the easiest of things to catch for the pot. Some people thought there was something in the air, in the water. Thomas, still working at the University, *had* to know more things than he let on ...

She went back home but could not sleep for thinking of the bird. She'd had hallucinations before, she could admit that much to herself. It was the hunger. She woke up in the middle of the night, unable to sleep, and went to the kitchen to make herself some hot water. She would have to make preparations to trap the bird. She had to find her, at all costs. She had to make sure she lived; she had to make sure she bred.

She could do this alone, of course. He would be a hindrance, she would be much more efficient without him goofing around ... But she flicked her little communication set and put the call out nonetheless.

Albert Ponsonby III walked back to his lodgings on the top floor of a triangular house, filled with narrow staircases and overheated passageways. It was a large house but extremely untidy, with a peculiar distribution of rooms due to its use as rental dwellings for young men who worked in the capital but could not afford any better. It was badly insulated and even worst lit, the home of mice, cockroaches and other creatures, which had got inside through its many cracks to escape the infernal heat only to end in someone's stomach.

Ponsonby was carrying several packages of different shapes and sizes: the synthetic coffee in one of the pink bags with its golden *Liberty* hologram, attesting that it came from one of the most exclusive shops still in business; the 'plastic' cheese, carefully wrapped in four conical packages of parchment paper, affecting the charming airship balloon emblem of the continental house *Fountaine*; a green glass bottle he had found and acquired as a present for Edwina to keep her boiled drinking water; and the most precious of his finds, the rare volume *Schleswig-Holstein Tages*, the book that Hobson, the nicer twin of *Hobson & Hobson*, had been able to procure for him.

Ponsonby negotiated with difficulty the mushy greenery spiked with fallen branches and the overgrown bushes that had taken over that part of the city. It wasn't easy to walk up the street, and he was forced to do so lifting his legs every couple of steps to overcome a new brambly obstacle—Ponsonby wasn't exactly fit. He reflected that Nature was getting very tiresome indeed, and he wondered why she was so persistent; she had so obviously won the battle against mankind.

The street was littered with abandoned vehicles, rotting in the scorched October sun: burnt, empty carcasses, which resembled the ruins of lost miniature civilizations. They served only one purpose now, as unlikely homes for colonies of lizards.

Albert fortified himself by thinking of the expensive treats he had managed to gather.

'Good evening, Natalia Fiodorovna.'

Ponsonby was never late with his meagre rent, but he had fought against any rise in the price with uncommon fierceness. It was clear to his landlady where his priorities lay.

'Humpff,' she snorted back, taking in the expensive-looking packages.

She had been living in the capital, one of the most developed colonies of the New European Coalition, for half of her life, and she had full command of the English language. However, she rarely chose to use it with Albert.

'Dear Madame Natalia Fiodorovna Kostkina, did you remember my ice?'

'Humpff.'

'In that case, thank you very much.'

Albert had the ability, acquired after many months of convivial existence, of interpreting the lady's grunts.

He faced the staircase with renewed courage. The promised ice had given him unexpected strength. Furthermore, he was carrying with him the invigorating promise of the food and, even more, of going to sleep by the sweet lullaby of the Baltic recipes of his new book —*pig's head, winter vegetables floating on the rich creamy milk of a Schüüsch stew, Fliederbeersuppe, infused with elderberry juice, with a light touch of olive oil, the broken sweetness of Bohnen und Speck* ... He would read them to himself out loud, an activity which would feed him for much longer than the synthetic cheese could.

He reached the last landing out of breath, and opened his door thinking about Edwina, imagining her delighted face when he gave her the glass bottle.

The green light was flashing in the communication system on the wall. A recorded message was waiting for him. The machine had been adapted years earlier from Albert's 50-inch internet-television set. Since his banishment from college, his father had refused to speak to him. Only two people called him now, Edwina and Thomas. If it was Edwina, he had the pleasure of admiring her face at a vast size; if it was Thomas, he was forced to witness how all his friend's features vibrated with animation while he recounted his many exploits in the Garden of Eden from which Albert himself had been so unjustly expelled. After all, the two remaining universities—remnants of a more glorious past, which nothing could end; for their vast, indecently acquired wealth made them as resistant to anything thrown at them as cockroaches were said to be to nuclear apocalypse—both were known to possess their own secret ways of getting food, something Thomas was always keen on reminding him.

He flicked the set. Bad luck. It was Thomas.

'Ponsonby! My dear chap!'

It was worse than he had imagined. Thomas was eating while he made the call. A delicious looking steak dripped juice as it hung suspended from a silver-plated fork.

'I thought you of all people would share my joy ...'

Share? Joy?

' ... at this particular moment. Behold, my gourmand friend! Behold, oh, connoisseur of all the delicacies of life! I am eating BEAR!'

Thomas's mouth opened grandly under his bulbous nose, magnified by the screen, as he took a bite. A smacking, ripping sound filled Ponsonby's room, contracting his stomach even more than it already was. He hated those 50 inches, each and every one of them.

'I feel like those hussars who fought with Napoleon, who were forced to eat the zebras from Moscow Zoo!' the gigantic head on the screen shouted.

This was beyond endurance. Why did Thomas insist on torturing him like this? He knew perfectly well that Albert had been expelled after the discovery that he had partaken of an illicit feast, by eating one of the remaining six deer from Magdalen College grounds. As Albert was tired of explaining, the creature was already dead when he stumbled upon the dinner party! Who could have resisted a little taste? He had only taken the daintiest morsel that could possibly be imagined.

'Rascal!' he cried to the intercom.

He flicked off the set. The green light still flashed; he had another message. Not even Thomas could be so tiresome. It *had* to be her.

His stomach contracted, in a completely different way this time.

The bright sun sent beams of light all over the place. He drew the curtains and flicked on the screen once more. Edwina's beautiful face appeared in majestic size in front of him, and Albert immediately forgot all the outrage he had felt only ten seconds before. He settled down to listen to his friend, his beloved, the object of his secret and all-consuming affection.

After Edwina's message was finished, he found himself shaking with a mixture of excitement, animation, and terror. Had his chance finally arrived to prove himself?

Edwina had also called Thomas, of course: he was a zoologist after all. But then, was a zoologist *really necessary* to catch a little bird? A wave of the old rivalry stabbed him like an electric shock.

Reluctantly, he put a call to Thomas to talk strategy. He only hoped that his friend had finished his luxurious meal.

After they had talked, he turned the room upside down looking for his grimy ABC Railway Guide. It would be the first time he would brave the slowly dying railway system in nearly nine months.

Wakefield didn't exist anymore. Neither the reserve, nor the Hall itself.

It was difficult to believe how quickly grand houses had crumbled into nothing once they had been abandoned. The notion infuriated Thomas. In those houses had unfolded a great part of English history.

The only thing that remained standing was the most delicate of all: the glass aviary, now emptied, intertwined with leaves and branches and filled with mud.

He was forced to walk the three miles from the train station, a plank of wood in the middle of nowhere, in the scorching morning heat. Norfolk was more humid than Oxford, due to the proximity of the sea, the sweating marshes, and the quickly advancing swampland with its cohort of new species. The flora was hardly recognisable. He hadn't been in this part of the world for a very long time, and things were rapidly changing. The trees gave the impression of being on top of one another, tumbled down or simply twisted, but this was misleading, due to the freakishly speedy profusion with which the new greenery had taken over. The bushes and the plants looked as if they could hardly breathe, one on top of the other.

He could make out King's Lynn in the distance, the church towers and the spires, and the little houses where families kept to themselves, still dazed by the all-conquering heat. The village's outline, those known buildings, sent a wave of memories of visits to Edwina, sometimes with Albert, sometimes on his own.

He went through the musky greenery, looking up at how the treetops form a vault over his head, like he remembered. Instead, he could only see the open sky, heavy with heat. He could smell the sea, almost hear the soft sound of moving water. What he couldn't find was the little stream: it had disappeared under the budding jungle, and it was only by chance that he stumbled upon the old remains of the kitchen garden and the house in ruins, with its line of bare trees and entry path.

A soft mist reached to where he stood, coming from the beach. He remembered it well; it was a horrid place, a vast, sublime expanse, with an oily and unmoving grey sea and a whitish, oppressive sky, colourless even under the bleached sun. The family of seals who used to live there hadn't been seen in years, according to Edwina; they had been claimed by the changes in the weather and the seasons, or perhaps killed and eaten. It was impossible to know.

He looked around. There was some uncanny beauty in this new world. A virginal meadow had sprouted as if from nowhere, the square traces of a formal garden still visible beneath it. The gossamer at his foot and the dry shrubbery inadvertently merged with the new, tropical forest. The leaves made a faint noise, gently rustled by the wind. There were hardly any other sounds, but he could smell the flowers and the tall shoots of young grass, and far away, as if in a dream, a cricket started his soothing noise. He reached to touch the flowers, caressed the tree trunks; a little dragonfly passed close to his face: granted, it was not exactly little ... the flying insect was as big as his fist, which was somehow spooky. But its beauty couldn't be denied. He felt at peace, in communion with that bit of land queerly overtaken by the peculiar greenery. Before he could help himself, he had put both arms around one of the bigger trees, and stood there, breathing deeply the purified air ...

A sound threw him out of his reverie.

It was some sort of groan.

His heart quickened, disconcerted at the interruption.

The male voice groaned once again.

He gently dislodged himself from his embrace of the tree, and gave a couple of noiseless steps in the direction of the sound.

There was a man squatting in the middle of the meadow.

Correction: there was a *priest* squatting in the middle of the meadow.

Correction: there was a priest *dropping one for king and country* in the middle of the meadow.

'What in heaven ...!'

The priest, realising someone had stumbled upon his most private moment, awkwardly put up his trousers and got up, with as much dignity as he could master. Looking around him, he stumbled towards the nearby brambles and disappeared.

Thankfully, Thomas had managed to hide at the last minute by catapulting himself towards one of the closest thickets. He got up, prickled by the unusual thorny leaves and, once he had satisfied himself that the priest had gone, he continued on his way to Edwina's cottage.

'My dearest, you have absolutely nothing to worry about!' Thomas spoke with the arrogance of a scientist. Albert let escape a long sigh. 'Let's be practical, shall we? What were the usual haunts of this bird, his natural habitat?'

'My dear fellow.' Albert could not stop himself. As usual, Thomas hadn't let him put a word across in nearly ten minutes. 'That is precisely the point! Their "natural habitat", as you so *scientifically* put it, doesn't exist anymore! For goodness sake! Have you seen the jungle out there?'

Thomas considered this with a smirk. Albert braced himself for a sharp reply. He would take it; he forced himself to remember that the old gang had reassembled with the sole purpose of helping his adored Edwina.

'Gentlemen.'

Both men composed themselves, and turned in Edwina's direction, grins blossoming in their faces.

'Please don't forget to give me your ration cards, otherwise I won't be able to get enough chicory for all of us while you're staying here.'

That settled the squabble.

They were sitting in the cosy sitting room of the cottage at the nature reserve, about half a mile from the ruined stately home. On the table, the rest of the durian soup, with its dollop of mock cream on top, reeked like a rotten corpse. Albert was thinking of the pink-footed goose, that little bird prancing around somewhere in the forest. And with that thought, some little red cabbage, white cabbage, came dancing after ... For goodness sake! He had to stop these images from creeping into his head! *Goose with red cabbage, goose with white cabbage, roasted goose, goose stewed with pears and wine with new potatoes and a tiny bit of brandy butter to go with each morsel, each bite musky and sweet.* His jaw bones were in pain now, and he started salivating ... Christ Almighty! He was there to help! He swallowed the forbidden images, and composed his expression. He forced himself to think about his new and wonderful book of culinary miracles, and recited in his head: *pig's head, winter vegetables floating on the rich creamy milk of a Schüüsch stew, Fliederbeersuppe, infused with elderberry juice, with a light touch of olive oil, the broken sweetness of Bohnen und Speck, Lübeck marzipan ...*

Edwina had started talking again. He looked in her direction, arranging his features into what he hoped was an intelligent expression, hoping that she had not noticed anything of what went on inside his head.

They decided on a course of action and went to bed early, nursing cups of rambutan juice. He fondled the hairy fruits, holding *Schleswig-Holstein Tages* close to his heart, trying with all his might not to think of goose with red cabbage.

Father Howlieberry had decided that there were some very odd goings on lately in his part of the world.

He was out foraging one morning, collecting rambutan and mushrooms and jackfruit, trying to decide how he was going to transport the forty-two-inch specimen he had found lying on the grass, when he saw them.

The two men were walking on tiptoe, one of them brandishing a butterfly net, the other awkwardly holding a small picnic blanket over his head. He went behind a tree, and peeped from his vantage point. The men were walking as in a dream, with deliberately slowness, until suddenly they lurched forward at the same point, and both fell flat on the nearby shrubbery.

The men got up and started gesticulating to one another animatedly, one of them pointing expressively at the bush they seemed to have tried to trap, and which obviously had not moved from its position, while the other threw his fists into the air in desperation.

'What were you thinking? I said "slowly"!'

'Ah! And what on Earth do you think I was doing, running a race?'

'Oh, Ponsonby ... We both know you are the one who wants to take the prize to the lady.'

'Don't you dare!'

'Your eagerness let the bird escape!'

The other man relaxed a little, and at the end they were both sitting panting on the grass. Neither of them looked particularly fit, or muscular.

'Bloody hell. We've been three days at it, and this was the first sight of the bloody thing!'

Father Howlieberry left at that moment, before he was spotted, not without first hiding his precious specimen of delicious jackfruit beneath a mound of gigantic leaves.

Later that evening, he was taking his usual stroll when he felt the call of nature. He moved towards his favourite spot, in the middle of the round meadow. He liked to be there surrounded by the large plants, with their characteristic strong smell, and something that resembled a willow tree but he wasn't sure what it was, from which creepers and bindweed hung in profusion. He positioned himself in the centre, unbuttoned his trousers, and set about his business, hoping for no other interruption like the one a few days earlier, when he had heard a male voice blaspheming in his direction.

Then he saw it.

Right in front of him, there were a few shoots of young wild asparagus.

They were green and erect and inviting.

And then a little feathered friend appeared out of nowhere, considering the green sticks.

Father Howlieberry did not move a muscle.

It was a bird. He couldn't see from where he squatted which kind of bird. A water bird, perhaps? It was too far away from the marshes. It looked like some kind of duck, but that was simply impossible.

It was a pink-footed goose.

Hadn't that woman said she had seen one?

It couldn't be!

He got up as slowly as he could, making as little noise as possible. He decided to stay close to the floor, and he crawled on all fours, hidden by the overgrown grass. He had to be fast and not make a noise, not an easy feat. Advancing was more difficult than he had imagined, and soon his elbows and his hands were scratched and covered in bits of grass.

He heard a strange sound he couldn't place ... A honk! It was a honk! Halleluiah! He hadn't heard the sweet sound in far too long ...

'Ponsonby! Over here!'

He could not believe his ears! Those fools again!

Goodness gracious! What were they doing now?

The bird was moving away more nonchalantly than could be imagined, and these fools were incapable of trapping it! He observed them making their awkward progress through the forest, wading through the grass like two clumsy bear cubs, putting up their legs as best they could, losing their footing and tumbling sideways with each step. They seemed to be sweating like mad in their stupid outfits, complete with hunter jackets and motorbike goggles, which only increased their ludicrous aspect.

'These fellows are not from round here,' he thought.

It was clear then that if anyone was going to get that bird into a pot it would be him.

They talked strategy over a lunch of leveret stew with thyme and radishes. The options were not many at that point. They had spent four days combing the area as best they could. They had seen the bird three times. The first time, they weren't ready. The other two, 'the characteristics of the countryside', as Thomas had put it, had made it impossible for them to trap her.

'My dear friends, perhaps it's time to admit that I will never have this bird under my loving care.'

Edwina had spoken with sadness, but also with a twinge of resignation. The two men looked at each other. It was obvious that they both wanted to jump at the opportunity to stop the charade. It was also obvious that neither of them was keen to be the first one admitting defeat.

'We could ...' Albert started tentatively.

'Perhaps ...' Thomas continued.

'Exactly ... It may be possible ...'

'Just what I was thinking, old chap!'

Edwina looked at them both in succession, a wave of disbelief crossing her features like a lightning bolt that made both men shut their mouths at once. Her faced contracted as she tried very hard to swallow the tears that were rapidly filling her eyes.

Without saying a word, she got up from her chair and left the room.

The two men stayed there saying nothing to each other for some time. Eventually Albert got up and started pacing the room, opening every little alcove, looking behind every single book.

'My dear fellow, what are you doing?'

'Looking for wine.'

'There's no wine left anywhere in the whole world!'

Albert sighed.

'I know.'

Edwina was lying in her darkened room. She had to accept it: the pink-footed goose had flown. She had been so close to trapping her!

To make matters worse, she was certain Albert thought she was a very silly woman. She had expected this visit to be the last one, to convince him to stay out here with her. But her longing for him meant nothing; it was clear he wasn't interested.

And, to add salt to the wound, now the pink-footed goosie had gone for good!

She would have to continue facing the future alone, without Albert, without the aviary filled with the species she would find, rescue, nurse back into the world. She had planned to use the excuse of needing help to run the whole aviary operation to ask Albert to stay. The goose had given her hope. It had been a nice dream. But dreams rarely come true.

Her own truth was somehow more complicated than she could ever admit, even to herself. She tried very hard not to think about it. She tried so hard that sometimes she could pretend that it hadn't happened as it did, but as she had reported it to the RSPB. The truth was, she hadn't been the last person to see a pink-footed goose; she had been the last person to see one alive. She had in fact killed the little creature.

It had been an accident, of course. The Jeep from the reserve was still running, and she hadn't seen the little goosie crossing that path. It was pitch dark. The bird should not have been there. At that time of day the geese were resting somewhere, wherever it was they went.

But the sad truth was that she had killed the last recorded pink-footed goose in the British Isles.

'So many creatures are not here with us anymore ... Animals that were alive only five years ago are now disappearing! Bees and sparrows and frogs and whatnot.'

Edwina was sitting on a rock, utterly exhausted. They had given themselves one last chance, and it had been useless.

In truth, Ponsonby did not mind that much the lack of little creatures in the planet, although he would never confess this to her. To him, the hardest truth to swallow was that he could hardly remember how some of them tasted.

They were standing close to the old orchard, and he recognised the pear tree, the plum tree, the apple tree, the gooseberry and blackberry shrubs, all dead now, rotten, dried down to their last ounces of life. He tried so very hard to evoke the taste of those fruits in his mouth, the soft meat of a ripe pear, the rich velvet of gooseberry jam ... It was useless, his memory did not retain an ounce of any of them. He could call up adjectives, ideas, but not the tastes, the smells. He couldn't recall a soft summer breeze, or August rain, its lightness conjuring up a musky, alive odour from the grass. The new, freakish downpours they endured during the rainy months, typhoons that broke things and tumbled down trees, only smelled of clay and dust and destruction. Of outlandish, bright-coloured fruits, rotting on the ground.

The bird was gone, there were no traces or signs of its presence anywhere in the forest. It was as if it had never existed.

Father Howlieberry gathered everything necessary, the bucket with water, a cleanish tea-towel, ancient yellowish pages of *The Times*. He chopped the wings off, first breaking through the bone, and then plucked the feathers slowly, one by one. It was better to do it like this, instead of grabbing handfuls. He remembered that much. Next were the neck and the two legs. Once they were gone, he opened a hole and extracted the innards. He collected everything, except the feathers, to make stock and blood pudding later on. Then he prepared the bird for roasting. He thought that it would be one more year at least until the electrical supply would be gone for good. He would have to make provisions to organise a wooden oven after that. Although it was more than possible that by then there'd be nothing left to roast.

He was forced to experiment, and cooked the bird with chunks of the jackfruit he had foraged. Soon, the cottage was filled with mouth-watering aromas.

An hour and a half later the bird was ready, and he had had enough time to work himself into a fit on anxiety.

He would go to Hell; that much was clear.

Who was he, after all, to deserve survival more than other human beings?

He knew where to find them. The woman's cottage was in the old reserve, less than ten minutes' walk. And they had been so keen on the catching the bird! It was decided: he would share his meal with them.

With this new resolve, Father Howlieberry found a lid for the Le Creuset roasting dish, wrapped it in teatowels and set off.

Edwina's sister and nieces lived in the capital, but she rarely visited them. He could hope to see her again in three or four months, if he was lucky. It was now or never!

Albert Ponsonby III didn't know what to do, a state of mind he was only too familiar with. It was difficult for him to make decisions, but once he was set on a course of action, he was also very afraid of putting his ideas into practice. He wasn't sure he could deal with rejection. At least, while he said nothing, he was safe. Safe, but without her.

He heard someone talking in the back garden and walked to the little window of his room. Thomas had put a hand on Edwina's shoulder; he was consoling her. Damn it! Why had he gone to his room? He was an utter fool! He wondered why those two didn't get together once and for all.

There was a knock on the front door. Thomas and Edwina didn't move. Reluctantly he went down. He wondered who it could be.

As he climbed down the narrow little staircase the knocking came again. It sounded strangely muted, as if someone was knocking with his head. He opened the door.

'Hello?'

It was a priest, holding a delicious-smelling casserole dish, and knocking with his elbow.

'Good evening, my friend!'

Albert was at a loss; something was very wrong indeed, he could feel it in his extremely delicate stomach. He looked at the priest face, then at the casserole, and something clicked.

'What on earth ...? What do you have there?'

'Oh, well. I had seen you trying so hard! It was easier for me, I know this part of the world very well; I used to hunt here with my father as a child.'

'*What?!*'

'My friends! Please share my meagre meal with me!'

To the priest's surprise, Albert came out and closed the door behind him. Edwina could not see this.

It was too late. Both she and Thomas had re-entered the cottage from the back garden, and were now following into the hallway to find out what was going on.

'What's wrong?' asked Father Howlieberry.

Albert tried to shoo him out, but the priest was having none of it.

Edwina was already out, sniffing the air with her delicate little nose.

'What is that smell?'

'My dear! Please accept this humble offering from your neighbour ...'

It was too late. Father Howlieberry had just opened the lid of the Le Creuset.

Edwina's eyes opened as wide as salad plates.

Her lips parted as if she were about to receive a large chunk of wedding cake.

Her nostrils kept quivering charmingly, as if she were tasting the nicest wine in the world.

Albert and Thomas turned in her direction, panicked expressions on their faces. The priest looked extremely confused, from one person to another, and back at his casserole.

Edwina opened her mouth even more; Albert braced himself for an inconsolable scream from the sweetest, most adorable creature still alive on Planet Earth.

'Oh, bugger,' she sighed at last. 'We might as well eat it.'

THE ICEBERG IN MY LIVING ROOM

*Sleep, little boy of mine,
sleep, I'll watch over you;
May God give you good luck
in this world so untrue.*
—Traditional Andalusian Lullaby

To Kathleen Rani Hagen

THE DOCTOR IS RECITING THE LIST; IT SOUNDS LIKE A SONG. Citalopram, escitalopram, fluoxetine, fluvoxamine, paroxetine, sertraline, duloxetine, venlafaxine, amitriptyline, imipramine, nortriptyline, alprazolam, chlordiazepoxide, diazepam, lorazepam, buspirone, isocarboxazid, phenelzine, selegiline, tranylcypromine.

The good news: I can still breastfeed with the stuff he picks out, after looking at my file on his screen for less than a minute. Win-win!

The bad news: I may have problems getting to sleep.

Bad news? That's a bonus, right? Who wants sleep anyway, when there is so much to do and absolutely no time to do it?

I wake up around five in the morning, while everyone else sleeps, and get to work. This is in fact the third or fourth time I've woken up: I am breastfeeding, of course. But the other awakenings haven't been for me, not really. Here I am, trying to do the impossible. I am trying to match my resumé to a new set of variables on a new set of job specifications. Behind me, my husband is snoring soundly. In the cot the baby stirs. I try to do all of this without breathing: if the baby wakes up, that's it. I'll have to stop. There are no two ways about it.

I am an old hand at this. I have done it now eighteen times. Someone once told me that they needed to apply to sixty-five jobs before finding a position. Sixty. Five. The number looms ahead of me, menacingly. I am not as resilient as this friend is. I worry I will not manage sixty-five applications. I worry I will not manage twenty. The rate at which I am losing the energy required to play this game is frankly outstanding. I am also quickly losing whichever focus I thought I possessed at the beginning of the process; whatever that was, for it is oh so difficult to remember ... Financial security? Self-worth? Status? Who the hell knows. I read again my so-called 'accomplishments'. They feel hollow, sound hollow. They are not more special than any other candidate's will be. They are probably useless in the context of this job. My past life mocks me now, all those things that were so difficult to get, so important that I get them, all that hard work for absolutely nothing, no gain, no prospects, of any kind. The Master's degree. The second Master's degree. The third Master's degree. My husband's boss has just been awarded her second doctorate. Two. Doctorates. That sobered me up, quickly. He was beaming when he told me, of course, wondering if getting her a card were praise enough. I panicked. Are we now entering a new era in which two doctorates will be needed? When I graduated, I was told I needed a postgraduate degree to teach, so I did one. By the time I was finished, what was needed was a doctorate, so I got one. Then I needed to publish one novel: I did. A couple of them. Three. Now, of course, I cannot find a job. Predictable.

Next, I look at my teaching. I have done everything imaginable, from language instruction to supervising dissertations in a variety of topics. At the time, I accepted those meagres—crumbs fallen from the adults' table—because I myself needed to eat. Ironic. Now, it seems that their only function is to highlight what little focus I have, how I am a master of all trades, which invariably translates as not being proficient in any.

Next, I look at my publications. I used to think that having one book published would make a difference. A game changer, you know. It didn't. I used to think that having two books would make a difference. I used to think that having three books would make a difference ... etcetera, etcetera.

Next, it is my statement of teaching philosophy. I cannot understand a word of it myself, so I wonder what others will get out of it.

These seven pages are telling a story, a story that could be mine, or someone else's. But they do not say anything about me, not really. They don't explain who I am, what I can do. They do not reflect my passion for teaching, how much I care, actually care, like a moron. I guess, on reflection, that is not the point. Funny thing: I didn't realise until now.

Wake up, little one. Wake up. Let me tell you a tale, the story of the Iceberg in my living room. This is also, now, your living room, little one. Wake up in a flash, so you can see the Moon, huge like a huge huge plate, shining through our window. The fire is on, the cocoa is hot for mama, the milk dips from my breast to your lip.

Suck, suck, suck.

And you, little one, are content. You, little one, fall asleep again. So wake, little one. Listen.

What is that thing? You ask. What is that thing, a black and white photograph, framed black on our mantelpiece? That solid cloud dancing on the bright bright Ocean. Is it a boat, mama, all white, all shiny? Is it a cloud, made of mother-of-pearl? Is it a mountain, perhaps?

That, my beloved, that, my sweet, that, my joy, is the Iceberg. What is an iceberg, you ask. It is not a cloud, it is not a boat, it is not a mountain. What you see is only the tip of it, inside the water it is like an upside-down tower. The ice pack. A mighty construction. I will tell you how it went. Those, my sweet, were the mighty keepers of water. We can only see the tip, no idea what is underneath, how much there is underneath ...

It has started: I am babbling now, making little sense. I become vaguely aware that my face is set in a manic smile, and that I am behaving in a manic way. There are five squares with five faces on them sitting on my computer screen, every single one of them looking at me enquiringly, worryingly, seemingly surprised that I turn out to be as I am. I can understand how they are feeling: I only got this interview because I applied under my husband's English name, so I am not at all what they were expecting. Will they see beyond that? Beyond my accent, my olive skin, my borrowed name? Will they see *me*? The eternal question.

'So, tell us. How would you manage giving one-to-one academic skills support to a variety of learners from a variety of backgrounds, coming from different cultures, speaking different languages, studying a variety of topics, on the actual hours of the appointment? After all, it is a part-time, nought-point-five full time equivalent.'

The Chair smiles genially at his own ... *Quip? Cruelty?* The other faces on the other square boxes, dancing on my computer screen, suppress a little, nervous laugh. I panic. How to give that kind of support with those working conditions, indeed? My reply, the one inside me, fighting to come out, is simply that you can't do it. Not in this part-time post, not with this excessive number of students. I shut my mouth in time: at least, this is not an hourly-paid position. I should be grateful I've got this far.

'Well ...' I start. I have nothing to go with that. A little cough saves me. Something floats in front my computer, a white shade of fluffiness. I cough for a few more seconds, profusely apologise, drink a sip from my glass. My hand is shaking, and the water makes absolutely no difference. I have prepared answers; I've prepared questions and have prepared answers. Not this one. At least, by the time I have drunk, I have come up with a reply that does not sound like a complaint. It is all very vague, too vague. More nervous laughs emerge from my computer screen. More manic grin on my face. My face is fixed. I am not a candidate anymore, but a set of teeth.

I am sitting in the living room, looking at the Iceberg. You have finished drinking the sweet milk, are mercifully asleep. For how long? We will see.

I need release. I lay on the floor, the ceiling above me. Would I manage to see through it, to become one with the shooting stars, to touch the stars up there, their maps of light and beauty? I close my eyes, very hard, and force myself to travel up, become one with them. Anything but here, this failure, which soon you will come to understand. Sweet escape! I run fast through the ether, fast through the sky. I am one with the dark and the galaxy and all the constellations shining bright; the stars shouting at me, saying hello.

Hello Moon! Hello comets! Hello stars!

Night is my friend, and I go up and up and up, let myself fall into her.

I fly so hard North that there is no way back. Where do I fly? To the iceberg in the picture. Of course. The iceberg on the picture, framed in black, that my husband gave me as a present, back in the days when I was young, back in the days when I was beautiful; back in the days when he still loved me, when he didn't want to sleep with others.

Why did he present me with this one, in particular? What does it mean? Does it mean that he intuited more to me that met the eye? Or does it mean that he expected more from me? What a failure I must be to him, what a disappointment. The same failure, the same disappointment that I am to myself.

Once the resumé is done, I need to write a covering letter. I need to write *another* covering letter. I need to write a 'new' covering letter, which will be a composite of all my previous covering letters, a collage of pretensions and half-truths, a patchwork of how interesting I can possibly make myself sound—all lies, of course—a mighty Frankenstein-letter, stitched up in ink and words and paper.

As soon as I land, I know the ice is my friend. The ice loves me, the ice looks after me. The ice engulfs me with its quiet calm. My feet are feeling the sting of the cold through my pink slippers; I am not wearing the right clothes. The packed ice is crunching underneath me. I have wanted many things until now. I have wanted wheels, so I could jump in and get away, as far as I needed to go, as far I wanted to go, and never feel trapped anywhere. I have wanted things, books and clothes, and pink slippers, so I could understand who I am again, remind myself of who I am. Books and clothes and security and a career. I have wanted a home somewhere, waiting for me, so I could feel safe, so I could feel that I belonged. I had wanted a living room, and in the living room a mantelpiece, and on top of it the print of a picture, an iceberg, perhaps, or some long gone thing that doesn't exist in our world any longer. I have wanted it all, craved it all. But I've never wanted the burden of things before. Why did I think they would ground me?

I am unable to sleep. The Moon lights up the room. I know, suddenly, what I truly desire. I have wanted you, little one, so badly. What took you so long?

The login doesn't work. If I don't write my students' reports before the deadline, I won't be paid. I won't be paid the meagre, below minimum-wage hour-rate that does not take into account all the preparation, normal levels of communication with my students, and all the admin that this entails, plus more admin, prim little admin cherries on all the admin cakes.

This unpaid time doing stuff around the teaching is what I hate the most; this unpaid time doing 'admin', 'scheduling', 'organising', and the endless 'emailing'— why is it, I wonder, that one little email, always, invariably, generates six more?—it is this that almost tips me over the edge. But I like teaching, I keep saying to myself, and I like my students. Four years of this. Because I like teaching, and I like my students.

Every single year I have to demonstrate the same things: I am worthy to be here, and yes, you can sign me up on a new hourly-paid zero-hour teaching contract. Yes, you can renew my login. Sorry to bother you, you have forgotten to renew my login. Yes, I will call IT myself. No, sorry, IT assures me that HR needs to give the all-clear, before they can do anything about this, so in fact you have to ... Yes, of course! My passport, again, scanned and delivered! It is no problem at all; although, if I may ask, why don't you have it on file, after all these years ...? No problem. Absolutely no problem. Wait, sorry to be such a pain ... Still not working. No, I am sure I tried to log in with the correct email. Yes, I have more than one email account, as any normal human being does who zero-hour-tutors all over the place ... No, I am not trying with the wrong email account. Yes, I will try again. No, it doesn't work. I understand how you think I may be wrong; so, here it is a snapshot of the message I am getting. Wait, it is the password which doesn't work now. Yes, I entered it correctly. No, sorry, here is another snapshot, to show you I am entering it correctly. No, you are not being patronising, not at all ...! Yes, yes, no worries. *I* will call IT again! No, I cannot try once more; it's blocked me now. Okay, I will try once more, just in case. Wait, couldn't it be this after all, that IT hasn't renewed my password this year ...? Ah! *That* was it. No worries IT, not trying to do your job. Sincere apologies! Although, I must admit, I am happy to have been correct, after three mornings wasted and thirty emails written in my copious, ever-expanding, sweet sweet sweet unpaid time ...

Many days and many hours later.

All that bloody admin, that creeps up and eats up my writing time, my living time, my with-you time, little one.

Still, I am teaching, am I not? *First world problems ...* How selfish can I possibly be?

Not to be dramatic, but ... I would take my eyes out with a fire poker just not to do that bloody unpaid admin ever again.

Finally, I manage a couple of hours of sleep between feeds. And it is beautiful: I dream, dream of being a bird. I try to sit up and fly. Only I do not fly. Instead, in my dreams, I lay an egg. It only has rage inside.

I am lying here now. I have arrived. I am one with the iceberg.

How incredibly peaceful it is.

I realise now, a very important thing. That the dark doesn't fall equally everywhere. That there is some certainty in this mighty ice, but not anywhere else. That those things my heart has secretly desired were all illusions.

I am one with the iceberg, I am one with the ice. The atoms inside me also forming capricious constellations, galaxies, the atoms which are the same atoms that form this planet, where this iceberg sits. Where my living room sits. Where all the things sit that are useless, desired for one minute, in truth unwanted. Because I only wanted you, you, you.

You suck at my breast, round like the Moon. Like the Moon white, like the Moon full. And I am contented. The stars around us are swirling this way and that one. But we cannot fly, the burden of things held us in place. The burden of things breaks the mighty ice. The burden of things melts it into nothing, water, thin air, a dream. The stars swirl, making this whooshing noise, and time and space become one. We are one with the iceberg. We are one with the Universe. From here, it is easy to see it all, so easy, our beginning and our end.

The system is so difficult to navigate, that one of my friends is suggesting the unthinkable: could it be so difficult, *on purpose* ...? Hang on. What would be the reason behind ...? Oh, I see. To make it hard to do the claims. Indeed, new contracts to sign with each hour of lecturing, or block of two, three hours at most. The system seems to have swallowed up one of these contracts, like the Tiger swallows up every single teacake in my daughter's favourite story. I am doing all the sounds this time, exactly as she likes it. With the swallowing comes a big *'Gwap!'*. And I think about my lost contract, my lost hours, in that labyrinthine system designed to look like the land of leaving and never coming back ... As soon as she is asleep, in the early hours, screen after screen after screen; I fail to locate this contract, which I am positive I signed, which I am positive was approved by the relevant departmental Baron. Oh, well. Oh, dear. Approved, or not approved, I taught those hours. Done and dusted. Although it now seems that, if I understand correctly, the two hours not being here, somehow, means that I can't be paid for them.

'Gwap!'

Many emails, many days, many weeks later.

Impossible to convince the department that they owe me money. Impossible to do anything at all about this. I won't be paid for these classes.

There are no more icebergs. They only exist in our imaginations, and as ours does, trapped in a frame, atop a mantelpiece. Pretty pictures. Or in drawings, or recordings, mechanical ghosts, soulless images. There are no more icebergs. Our love was not enough, love doesn't tend to be. Something else is needed, apart from words. Actions. Policies. Forcing your way in. How innocent we were, my love. We lost it all, and, for you, I would travel back in time, back in space, back in atoms ... Too late, I hear you say, in between your suck, suck, sucking.

Daughter, don't hate us, for we didn't know what we were doing. Or did we? A friend of ours used to say: blame the Russians! If they hadn't messed it up so royally, perhaps capitalism would not have become the God it did ... Really? The Russians? Still, she must know what she was talking about: she became a Professor somewhere elite, somewhere Ivy; one of the two. You know what I mean.

Sleep, little one. I wanted you so much that I think I imagined you into being.

I think of that poem, often. I imagine that, indeed, razors pain you. Rivers *are* damp. Could I even get hold of any acid? Guns are, thankfully, not lawful in this country, or at least not easy to get. I could not manage to make a good noose, who does? Gas stinks, right? In any case, the drugs, the drugs ... They used to be my friends. When I was younger, when I was beautiful. Not anymore. Not now you are there.

The doctor was wrong: I have been sleeping! Or at least existing in that dreamy state, between being sleep and being awake. Sleep mixed with feedings, feedings mixed with exhaustion, exhaustion mixed with the same repetitive task that every time is slightly different, slightly the same; as if I were conjuring a new parallel timeline with every application, with every resumé. And in every timeline, it is so exhausting to live.

My dreams are strange.

Is it too clichéd to say that they seem too real?

After dreaming that I laid an egg, I woke up from a dream of flying, of freedom, with dreams of being a bird. But I wasn't a bird. I was a dinosaur. How did I know. I had dinosaur feathers, they were thick and lustrous. They were powerful.

And like that it ends, as it all ends, as the Iceberg ended, and now it rests, alone in my living room. Stuck in a black frame. Forever sleeping, sleeping ...

Fox & Raven

Look before you leap.
—'The Fox and the Goat'

1.

THERE IS A SPECIFIC BURNT SMELL THAT EMANATES FROM the kind of farming that Fox preached as the ultimate sin of humanity. People worked the land, and they would accumulate debris; or perhaps a field would need to be cleaned in preparation for opening wounds in the earth. The burning would come later, huge mounds of stuff that needed to be disappeared. This was something they often used to do at her grandparents' place; children dancing around the flames, a moment of delight. Knowledgeable adults worked the mound and the flames, moving stuff, adding more, making sure it was all kept safe. Even under the control of old hands, the flames elongated against the purple sky, at times shot out a scary arm towards someone, as if they were trying to get at them.

The children were told not to get near the fire, suggesting a power that was difficult to parse. They could sense the fascination it created in the adults. Her sister wasn't born yet. Louisa was still alive.

This was all before everything important had happened: before Louisa had passed, and her father had got her and Ginger and taken them to join Fox.

Now, driving along the Suffolk coast was like travelling inside a scorched landscape. It was difficult to ignore: it was exactly the same smell as those joyous mornings, but it meant exactly the opposite. They had no television in the compound, and she and Ginger had missed it terribly. But there were radios, and they used to be on while the adults performed their duties. From scorching summer to scorching summer. From reporters using the expression 'tinder-box conditions' for the first time, to the very real possibility that the fires they saw happening in Mediterranean countries from May to September—so very far away, happening to others, never to them—would finally reach them. Were those countries *really* so far away?

She remembered the first time she saw a neat row of English suburban houses burning down. Someone had decided to set up a barbecue in a garden, the green and pleasant land of his lawn turned yellow by the heatwaves and the drought; the barbecue man still cheerful because it was sunny. Beautifully ignorant, they had all been. And now, here she was, driving deep into the scorched land. Everything she saw ahead was black and cinders. But the smell. The smell was exactly the same as those years ago, reminded her of children dancing and playing. She could not help but find it strangely comforting.

'Do you think we'll see a dog today?' Her sister had been lured away with this one promise, this one lie. Still, better a lie than staying at Fox's.

'Sure, we'll see a dog today.'

She saw Ginger's face screw up in disbelief. Her sister was eight years younger, but she was no fool. At times, Raven thought Ginger could see through her, straight through her.

Raven's real name wasn't Raven, of course. This was the name Fox had given her, so many years back. She just didn't remember what her real name had been, and now she was stuck with this strange fanciful identity.

She knew vaguely she had been named after her maternal grandmother. She hated her maternal grandmother. They had last visited her on their way to Fox's, all those years ago. Louisa had passed—she always called her mother Louisa, even in her mind—and her father stopping at his in-laws' house, and her grandmother making them enter through the back door, and feeding them on the kitchen table, and not allowing them anywhere else in the house. She had been barely eight years old, but her grandmother had chastised her about the correct use of cutlery and her table manners. Ginger had cried. Her father had taken them out of there as soon as possible. When they got to the compound they were joyously received: they had been expected. Fox himself came out to greet them; it was a rare honour. She recognised him immediately: this was Fox, the famous Fox! He had been to visit, all the way to Scotland, had introduced himself as their father's college friend. The two men had sat and talked for hours. Fox was tall and gangly, blonde and with an elongated face that ended in a pointy chin. His blue eyes looked through you from beneath raised eyebrows. He had smiled at her, at Ginger. They had showed him their pride and joy, their collection of small plastic figurines.

The visitor had grown strangely silent at this, and their father had started apologising on their behalf. Ginger and Raven knew they had done something wrong; they just couldn't work out what. The visitor had walked out. Louisa had looked at the scene from the kitchen window: their visitor contemplating the sunset over their fields, and their father running over to him, gesticulating. Eventually, the two men had embraced, and returned to the house.

Their father had explained to them that the figurines were wrong, evil. And then he had taken them away, at the same time purging all plastic toys from the house. Truth to be told, that hadn't left them a lot.

Only then had the visitor agreed to enter the house again.

2.

They fish for pearls in the depths of space was what Fox had preached. And she was hooked, to him, to his words. Would it be true, that one day they would go and find pearls together? How was she to know that one day their father would go there first and leave them behind, mourning? Well, not mourning. Fox did not allow mourning.

'Come,' Fox had said to her. He took her hand and put it at the back of her father's neck to show her it was still warm. Was it?

But she knew it: he had gone, long before they got there. And she had missed saying goodbye.

It had taken Fox and Raven a few hours to arrive: the drive out of Fox's own private compound by the coast had been longer than she remembered. It was one of those hot nights at the end of September. The mosquitoes crashed against the windscreen; weeks later, their corpses would remain, gluey spots of brown and yellow on the dusty glass. The night itself seemed to chew on the air, heaving. Fox concentrated on steering the car, riding deeper into the hot darkness. From time to time he put his hand on Raven's thigh, and left it there for a few seconds, just long enough to remind her that she was still his. His choice bride.

The lights of distant towns glimmered, yellow and orange, lives lived the wrong way, not Fox's way. He was handsome. Did she think him handsome? He was a bit younger than father, had grown a powerful strawberry-blond beard. He was driving the car mechanically, she knew he wasn't thinking about her dad, or about her. He was musing on other more important matters.

The caravan park at the edge of the communal compound held the old and infirm. Inside her father's caravan, a powerful smell of rubbish. It was impossible to know how long he had been dead. 'Come,' Fox had said, taking her hand, forcing her to do something she did not want to. Or had she? It was so difficult to know by now, to discern between one and the other.

Later that evening, Raven stepped out for some air. She always went out to look at the stars before going to their room, before getting into Fox's bed. It was then that she saw it: her little sister's constellation. The stars danced on the sky, as if sending her a message. And she understood. Fox had been planning to leave Raven there, if not now, at some point. He had been discussing keeping the caravan empty, for whom? It had to be for Raven. Was he going to abandon her there? Maybe not today, but, as always, Fox was anticipating the future. He was good at doing that. His whole system of belief was built around doing precisely that.

She went back to him, ready to beg. She would plead if she had to. Anything, everything, to remain with Fox, to be chosen bride. Anything, everything, so Ginger did not have to.

3.

They found a house. It was easy to see it was abandoned. Empty property always had the same attributes: overgrown gardens, nature starting the reconquest in her own messy way. Some boarded windows, apart from spaces people had opened to get in—she didn't let this put her off: there was an honour code among nomads like them. Were they nomads now, she and Ginger? It was difficult to know. All she knew was that she had needed to run, as fast and as far away as possible. There was some food still available, and hidden in the cellar, under an old blanket, neat rows of big five-litre water bottles. Bingo. She inspected them carefully with her flashlight before putting herself through the effort of carrying them upstairs. Miraculously, this lot didn't seem to have developed bacteria. She would boil it for Ginger anyway.

They settled down in front of the old laptop to an improvised meal of opened tins. She would try to get some animal protein, tomorrow. Ginger was licking condensed milk directly from a tin.

'Careful, you'll cut your tongue.' But her sister smiled maliciously and said nothing. She was enjoying herself.

They returned to the movie they had started watching the day before, downloaded from the ether.

'Do you think they were *that* big?'
'They must have been.'

They both stared at the screen, eyes glued to the creature of their childhood dreams. But Ginger, she said nothing. They were silent for a moment. The creep in the movie, the guy who sent the anonymous emails, had, of all things, a dog.

Dogs in old movies always surprised Raven: they both fascinated and disgusted her. She could not get over the way they moved about the scene, as if trotting, pouncing up and down a little, tails wagging, and those perennial smiles. Ginger was equally fascinated with the dog on the screen, as fascinated and as disgusted as her older sister, Raven could tell. Raven picked old movies carefully for Ginger. They were always from the end of the twentieth century, movies that her mother might have watched, perhaps, as a young girl licking her own tin of condensed milk. This was something they always said to each other. She might have watched this one. Why not? And the one they were watching now, a bizarre rendition of a scary pre-supra-connected world, with no notion of digital trace, imagined a sort of invisible virtual existence where it was possible to write anonymous emails. Ginger was enjoying the dog coming and going; Raven was wondering if this was suitable viewing for her little sister. There was something strange in the world depicted in these old movies, the streets filled to the brim with people—was it really like that?—shops where you could actually buy books, not just scavenge them out of deserted schools and abandoned libraries. And here, the possibility of a romantic relationship whose anonymity would surely generate death threats, harassment, murder. Sending and receiving emails to an unknown person? Telling them your innermost secrets? Raven couldn't conceive anything scarier than that, more stupid. Even living with Fox made more sense to her.

When had she grown to be such a cynic?

She guessed it was Fox's fault. Like everything else.

'This is sick,' she muttered. But Ginger kept glued to the screen no less, to the disturbing possibility of that happening, of it having already happened.

The last time they had seen Fox he had been running after their car, his scary face on, saliva flecking from between his lips. Ginger had been laughing, as if it was all a dream, the funniest of dreams. Then they had gained mile after mile after mile.

She wasn't sure how much time they had gained by stealing the car and abandoning Fox in that wood. He didn't have any form of communication with the compound; all of that was strictly forbidden. So he must have walked back there first, before coming in pursuit. Then again, had he decided to go after them? On good days she imagined he had probably thought, *why bother?* And then she remembered his pride, his stubbornness. Fox would never admit to be wrong. And she *had* been his chosen bride. And Ginger was due to become his next.

She was sure he would come after them; he had to.

And if he found them, they were as good as dead.

She was sure she had seen him, from time to time, staring at them from the edge of the road, staring at them from behind the windows of abandoned shops. This was not possible, of course. He could not be in so many places at once. Or could he?

4.

She remembered the first time she saw the miracle. Fox turning into a Fox. Until that moment, she had been sceptical.

They were in his private compound, a few miles from the communal one. She had been surprised to find so many forbidden luxury things there. Screens, although maybe they did not work. Old magazines and papers. He even had music, that he played from something she dimly remembered, called a Hi-Fi.

The other thing the compound had was privacy.

He brought her a dress to get changed into. It was white and floaty, but ripped in parts. It had red stains. Was it blood? For something to do, she remembered that old TV show she used to watch with Louisa, as a little girl: *was it cake?* Nope, this was real enough. This was happening. This was happening now. And suddenly the fear was so intense she almost blacked out.

She was special, she was chosen. Raven and Fox. Fox and Raven. When he walked towards her for the first time, before she passed out on the huge corner couch, she saw him clearly in her mind's eye: he was turning into his namesake animal. She could see the whole horrid scene from above, from the sides, from anywhere except her own eyes. As if she had abandoned her physical body. And all she saw was herself playing with a little fox. Of course, when she came round, something very different had taken place.

5.

She had been by the caravan park before, and she remembered: her head dizzy from the drag she had taken on that illicit cigarette. She was still little, attending lessons. But not little enough not to have seen the fox. The story she heard that day also made her dizzy, and slightly faint. She feared that any second now she might vomit. It was the impossible story of the end of days, as Fox called them. People were hungry, very hungry. So they ate the zebras at the zoo. And the giraffes, and the ostriches.

The old woman talked and talked and talked. They were in front of pictures of giraffes, pictures of ostriches, pictures of zebras. Rosie, the previous bride, was sucking her Coke from a can, through the hole between her front teeth.

The old woman talked to them as if they were children. But they were not children anymore, not quite. Rosie had moved to the caravans by now, they all knew her monthly blood was not stopping like Fox had hoped. The woman was saying that the place reeked still of animal, of fear. It smelt rancid, horrid, but Raven couldn't tell if it smelt of animals. It smelt like nightmares would, if they smelt. She instantly felt at home.

Rosie pressed her hand—she obviously did not like the place. She was too old by then to play with dolls and water the flowers in front of her mum's Virgin Mary, one metre of shiny, forbidden, horrid plastic, glowing with a multicoloured halo, its insides a long, humming bulb. She used to say it made her hot to the touch as well, comforting. She liked offering candles to her.

That day, in front of the pictures of the zebras, Rosie started to cry, and nothing would make her stop. Raven thought she was scared. Not of the absent animals, their feral smells, or the iron bars. Raven was the only one to understand why she was crying. She wanted to shout the obvious, *they ate the zebras!* But if she misbehaved, she would not come out next week to the lesson. Perhaps she would be sent permanently to Fox, instead of now and again. So she said nothing.

Perhaps Rosie was crying because her dad was long gone, leaving her mother with too many worries and a fetish for red candles lit to the Virgin Mary: her long chipped nails, baby pink like her roses, baby pink or red.

They were rushed to the bus, the lesson was over, and Raven felt dizzier than ever. With one hand on the vehicle she bent over, and it all came out in seconds. Why did she always need to puke in the mornings? When had this started happening? Since she had played with the fox. Was she sick? Would she be exiled to the caravans soon? At least after vomiting she felt so much better, so much better.

6.

That was the night it happened. Raven holding her breath, although the compound's alarm sirens were as faint as a ghost's whisper: Rosie's ghost, perhaps, calling her name. *Raven, Raven.* She was waiting for the sound of the alarms to die. They were tucked in their beds, she and Ginger, protected, deep underground. Rosie had only had a tin roof between the world and herself, between the flames and herself. Raven and Ginger, they were scared of nothing. Rosie was scared of the world.

Afterwards, there was nothing to bury. Rosie and her mother had been in the caravan, sleeping soundly from toil and hope and exhaustion. The rain was falling over the tin roofs, *drop, drop, drop*, over the black hole where the caravan was—a giant ashtray with a metal thing crunched into brown charcoal by the fist of God, or perhaps Fox, tinderbox conditions—and the roses, and the broken china, and the metre long Virgin Mary of multi-coloured, translucent plastic. There was nothing to bury, only the black dust and a family picture, and a red and white Coke can made from red and white carnations for Rosie, as tall as she had been. She loved her Coke. They left it out there, to get all soaked with the rain.

The next night Raven had a dream: the zebra was looking at her, black buttons for her eyes. Raven reached out to touch her, and she realised that she had sugar on the palm of her hand, at the ready, as always happens in dreams. The zebra ate it all up ravenously.

She was brave enough to caress her face, and it was the softest thing that she had ever known.

7.

As always, Ginger had seen through her, as if Raven was made of glass. Her real intention was to leave Fox behind, not to find a dog. And now Ginger was scared of dogs anyway. No more old movies!

Raven had always been always a curious child: she was also looking for answers. Aren't we all? She had to reconcile the way she lived with whatever was going on in her elders' heads: there was a dissonance between A and B. She could not name it as such, but she perceived it all the same, instinctively she could tell it was there.

Their lives had been shaped and reshaped, not by clear and serious events, but by diverse narratives, whatever it was that they had been told from certain channels, YouTube videos. She remembered how her father had his TV set directly connected to the ether at some point, what was called 'internet', so he could feed from these videos every day. He had stopped watching news: by then it was not possible to see what was rigged and what wasn't. They would spend hours sitting with his pals on camping chairs by the door of the HomesteadPrepp local. The shop, with its neat rows of 10-year cans of food, its low-level military paraphernalia, its bug-out bags, was our sort of community centre. And they, kids, would run amok on the dirt-road street playing that they were militia trained in aiming and shooting and all the rest of it, their impeccable training helping them discern seamlessly what was what, who deserved to live and who did not. They were so damn good at that, oh God. You have no idea how good they were. So they did what they were told, for years and years.

Eventually, Raven's parents dug their own bunker in their back yard, waiting for the pandemic to end all pandemics. After all, the Government had decreed it their own responsibility, they were not going to look out for them, they needed to do the work themselves, if they wanted to survive. If they intended their wives and husbands and grandparents and children to survive. Because it was coming, you know, it was always coming. Or the North Koreans would explode a nuke in the stratosphere right above them, killing off their electricity, and millions would die. Other countries—Sweden, Norway, Switzerland—had prepared underground protection for their millions of citizens ... Her Scottish father felt tricked. How could the British government be so uncaring? Her father could not really afford any of the bunker-kits that other people brought to their properties by boat all the way from companies in Dallas, Texas. From Vermont, from California. Really state-of-the-art things. Instead, he bought an old freight container and buried it, fitted it with an air filter that he got on eBay—Louisa was an expert at eBay, an expert at finding the best bargains, and knowing when exactly to bet to get them at the price she wanted.

The dugout was legendary for the children. They had seen it built up, or rather built down, mesmerised, and now it remained there, empty and dark, awaiting the end of days. At the time Fox came to visit, no one had ever slept in it.

In the end, her father had brought them there, to mum's England. To Fox. Fox had made him see: his clever invention would not save them. Only he could do so. Father was tired of waiting; he wanted the real thing. Raven understood at last: he did not know what he was doing, not really; but he had to do something. Taking some sort of action made it all mean something, anything. He had probably not anticipated that he would have to give his own daughter in exchange. Raven wondered if he had really escaped, like Fox had promised would happen when he took the pills. Or if what they had done was simply kill him. She had no hopes that her father had understood what he had done, to her, to Ginger. No such luck. He had surely died as stubborn in his ideas as he had lived.

8.

So, Ginger fears dogs. She is screaming now: there is a dog in the yard!

Finally! A dog! Raven rushes to the window; it's not a dog. It's a fox.

Fox has found them, and they are as good as dead. Or maybe he will take Ginger for his bride, will spare her at least. No such luck for Raven.

Raven understands at last: Ginger is not scared of dogs, she never was. What she is scared of is foxes, of course.

Bluebeard Variations

> *What a woman does is open doors*
> *It is not a question of locking and unlocking*
> —Joanna Newsom

1. the house

She yawns in the fog, stretching up to the sky.
A yellow dirt road runs between her and me.
Appearances are deceptive
from where I stand
she seems the gothic ruin of a gothic castle,
turrets, greenhouses, gargoyles,
the unreal air of prison, refuge, cloister.
Here I will be Teresa in her ecstasy,
Beatrice in her martyrdom.
Here I will reign
(briefly, painfully)

overseen by the gargoyles, the turrets,
a collection of closed doors, rooms shaded
by curtains eternally drawn,
and thousands of locks with thousands of eyes.

II. dolls

I wake up early to Judith's sobbing;
you are no longer here.
You have gone up to the study, your work,
leather-bound books and Bartók.
I cannot move,
I cannot get up.
I am a dead weight
unmoored in the middle
of the vast house. The house,
a gigantic compound eye at your service.
I know that you, alone in the study, watch me.
No one told me about this. What they said was:
nausea, vomiting, dizziness, holes in my teeth,
fingernails broken and ruined. They said:
foul cravings. And you, famous *gourmand*,
made to watch me eat jars of redcurrant jam,
stinking Marmite, chips.
Aches, sickness, terror of the birth.
Violent delight, fear.
That was all. No one said anything
about seeing the dead.

Now they visit I understand you;
everything fits in its proper place.
The collection of dolls, useless broken objects,
this out-of-control accumulation of junk.
The house, a gigantic eye with little eyes inside.
Dolls' eyes, mannequins' eyes.
You inherited these objects,
inherited the urge to dig them up—
antique shops and house sales,
grand houses brought to ruin like your own.
Gentlemen getting rid of their treasures, their
    favourite toys;
and you come back, the car filled with arms and legs,
stuffed birds, mechanical dolls,
kaleidoscopes, magic lanterns, philosophical games.
The entrance hall becomes an improvised field
    hospital,
and I remember that you were
in the faraway war, in a faraway land.
A war I know of from old wives' tales.

The singularity
that hangs about you
because you came back.

I don't think that the dolls are watching me,
but I do believe that they have conquered the place.
You smile when you fix one.
Impossible unworking collection of trash
    eccentricity.

Nothing like Vaucanson's duck, failed attempts at
    perfection;
unexpected anxiety.
What makes *me* more human than these rusty toys?
Not that much.

I am hungry. The girl inside me is hungry.
Guilt-hungry, fear-hungry.
What do I fear? Precisely this:
seeing them. Not seeing them.

You could play real tennis in this kitchen, such a huge
    cave, dank,
sunk underground in your castle of Never Return.
But there is nothing to eat.
The cupboards are bare, a cobwebby larder.
The stove as cold as our marriage bed.
No pheasants hang from the hooks in the ice-house,
no corpses, no pain stored inside.
A cold room—huge, hollow and useless.

Don't go in there, you say, *woodworm,
and the all-conquering and tenacious damp of centuries.*

Heavy shadows on the mirrors, all your beautiful
    women,
silent and mouldering and covered in dust.
I burst out laughing: when I see one it is always a doll
instead of the Hungarian opera singer,
the North American heiress,

the spiritualist with the palindromic name.
I don't understand the empty ice-house,
the pristine biscuit tins polished so brightly I can see
    myself.
I don't understand why there is no food at all,
as if you were saving ingredients for a more elaborate
    feast.
You go out hunting, you come home.
I don't know where you hide the little corpses,
dry blood staining your jacket,
and that glint in your eyes,
glossy as they sometimes are when you look at me,
as if you were about to cry
(sorrow? happiness?).

Wolves' eyes when they see their prey,
the instant before they spring.

III. POV: the first wife

Be bold—be bold; but not too bold.

She will come in now,
pause on the threshold for a second,
unsure whether to believe what she has seen.
Is it possible? she will ask herself.
She will realise, finally, that the silence of the house
    is a false silence,
now that her eyes are accustomed to the dust and
    the dark,

the rounded shadows, nooks and corners,
and can make out the abandoned spiderwebs,
the stains on the stainproof carpet.
If she has made it here, it is because she has seen
    the stuffed birds,
our sad menagerie of faded feathers,
dusty junk which someone at some point called
    'antiques',
the wax figures, life-size arms and legs
nothing more
than props for a lunatic,
(versions of womanhood, who used to be so exquisite,
who used to wear,
silent in the shop windows,
such beautiful dresses),
phantasmagorias.
If she has made it this far, she will be worried.
The 'curiosities' will drown her for an instant:
    unexpected anxiety
What makes her, in his eyes, more human than
    the toys?
Not that much, I hear her think.

How long I have been trapped in this porcelain coffin, with its pink cheeks and copper hair, from which I can see everything? All of them, I have seen, hands running over the wallpaper, unaware of the irregular beat of their hearts. Some open their eyes and turn them towards the doll, buried in the crystal urn. If I make enough of an effort, they see me then, the lines and curves of the word I have traced in the dust: *RUN*. Some faint, some look for him: already too late. They feel him, come upon them in an instant, eyes bloodshot, the poker held miraculously high over his head, sweat and saliva that he spits out with the effort mingling with that other, viscous liquid, which is brownish in this light instead of red, and which marks the end of the act and the curtain falling. Like one of those games: murdered in the wonder-room, with the poker, the act carried out by the doll-collector, hunter, piquet-player, lord of the manor, expert in Mahler, *etcetera etcetera* ... (ungrateful teenager, child-cat-torturer, wailing baby and, finally, black hole of nothingness, to which all of us must return). *Run away, disappear. Don't become another addition to our garden of turned earth. Darkness in the library, champagne pinching your tongue, the dull smell of the sempervivum, and love, all that you should know instead.*

IV. the locked room

There are thresholds it is better never to cross,
rooms which should stay sealed.
Vestibules, alcoves, wonder-rooms,
perverse collections of memories and dreams.
There are keys that can lock doors shut,
mid-sized keys, tiny keys,
keys with bows as enormous as bulls' eyes.
Heavy keys for cellars, catacombs;
thin keys for the breakfast room and the larder.

Rusted iron keys, bright aluminium ones,
bronze and gold keys for the secret chests.
There are *papier mâché* keys you offer me
with exaggerated courtesy,
but which I know to be useless.
There are other keys, made of memory and pain.
There are keys made of flesh and bone.

v. the dead wives

They came back yesterday,
their bluestocking know-it-all faces.
Very quiet, all of them,
like broken dolls at the foot of my bed.
They seem to understand that I cannot have the
    girl.
They seem to know the future, all pasts.
The present is this house, the dolls, them,
and all the doors that should never be opened.

vi. the end

A silhouette. So beautiful she looked like a doll. The new wife did not want to breathe so that the vision would not disappear: so many questions she had on that moment, curiouser and curiouser. *She checked that she was not feverish, that she did not feel bad, so there was no possible excuse, no physical reason that might interfere with her encounter with the beyond.*

The dead woman shivered. She seemed cold.

She wanted to go upstairs to tell him, but he had left instructions that he was not to be disturbed, there was a lot for him to do that day, like any other day. She was never to come into his room, she was not to go into the doll-room. Absolutely never.

He was not to be disturbed under any circumstance, even if it were a matter of death, even if it were a matter of life.

At the Museum

*The origin of the modern museum is linked
to the development of the guillotine.*
—Georges Bataille

I TRY TO UNDERSTAND THE MUSEUM. I TRY TO PUT together the pieces. It is a collection of dormant feelings, preterite situations. There are the bones of animals there, reminding us of what was lost, but what drew you to its chambers was something different, the things which we have extirpated from our experience. I remember you, think about you. You loved shadows, so you loved the Museum. The first time I entered it was with you. I went numb at the vastness and the profusion of objects. I felt privileged. How many had ever had access to this collection of absent things? The vast reception chamber resonated with the echoes of our steps. From the ceiling hung the dessicated heart of the extinct blue whale, also sextants and quadrants, with complicated calculations painted on them. But you were not interested in any of these showpieces. You were here for the shadows, the heart and soul of the Museum. Next to this forbidden lore, and beyond the abundance of things, on a vaulted ceiling painted in black, shone the cosmographies, marking the path we must wander. At the hour of the crows the cosmographies lighted up, filling the space with their magical tapestry of meaning. I was capable of recognising some of them, the ones all the children learnt by heart. My own constellation: the Hare. The Librarian. The Fox. The Bird-Ascending. They were here to protect us, to keep an eye on us, so our minds did not wander among the vanished objects.

The Museum is filled with dangerous ideas, that is what you said.

I had never seen the cosmographies so clearly as on that first night at the Museum. Each of them told an authorised story. At dawn, we went up to the vaulted forest and fell asleep among the gigantic roots of the *Dracaena draco*. No one saw us, or so we thought. You told me then of those antiquated emotions that are forbidden us, as extinct as the whale. Primitive practices, thankfully gone. You spoke of your own fabrications, immersions designed to find a path again towards them. You spoke of forbidden, heretic things. I was frightened and fascinated by your words in equal measure.

What are you working on now? I asked. So, you told me. This shadow was particularly difficult to understand. You invoked words that had faded a long time ago, disappeared with finality. The shadow itself, its purpose, could not be explained, it had to be experienced. I agreed to go into the simulation.

A man travelling in an unknown land, sleeping in an unknown bed. Something happens in darkness, and something is revealed, not alive but not dead either. This had been your own simulation, your *first* simulation. And as such it was imperfect, untamed. It wasn't accepted for the collection, and so it lingered in your home, unwanted. At times your friends would come and plug themselves in. We would be intoxicated with the steam of the green anemone, pretending to have dreams and visions, we who had no notion of ideas forming inside our heads outside of the simulations themselves. You were now talking about yet another blasphemous thing from the past. You described it thus: the eyes follow the letters on something called a page. Somehow, you explained, the brain transformed the meaning afforded into moving images, directly inside. You invoked the possibility of gaining knowledge by this primitive method; we were shocked at you and your provocative ideas. It was thrilling to hear you talk about those preterite things. Working for the Museum allowed you a modicum of freedom to do so; but we also knew that any minute the crows could enter your compound and enslave us all. We were fearless, intoxicated not so much by the anemone as by your own reckless behaviour, your ill-advised notions: we run simulations to make us feel, because we have forbidden ourselves to feel anything and we cannot remember how to do it; we run simulations of Nature as it was, because it has not been as diverse since we humans deliberately finished it off; we run simulations of everything that has been lost, because the Museum is a grand simulation in itself, one that pretends that we understand everything, when we do not understand anything.

He stops at an inn. The owner takes him up to an attic bedroom, located right at the end of a steep staircase. It is rather inaccessible, but it has its own bathroom, and a bed hard as stone that he accepts as though it were the most comfortable he has ever slept in. On the little table there is a jar and bowl to wash your face, and next to the cloudy mirror, a little Saint card, and a little upside-down bouquet of dried flowers. Over the bed there is a wooden cross, and in a corner a little triptich, also made of wood, representing the annunciation, with candles and dead flowers. But it is the bouquet that conveys the most meaning for him. He guesses that, the inn being completely full, he has been given the little bedroom of one of the owner's daughters, who will probably have to sleep with a sister, or even the horses. He feels sorry for the girl, but it is late and he is exhausted.

It is already dark when he lights up a candle to go down the narrow staircase to the main dining room, where he is served a stew of venison, potatoes, and vegetables, with the boiled liver of some other animal. After the meal is finished, or after at least he has eaten as much as he is capable of eating, he goes back upstairs, gets into bed, and sleeps.

He dreams: he is on the shoreline he saw while driving along the road towards the inn, sitting on one of the dunes scattered with dark, lank grass. There is a girl down on the beach, and from there she is indicating to him he should come closer. He gets up. But it is she who floats his way, not walking, exactly, but sliding somehow, unnaturally, over the sand. She goes so fast her feet do not touch it; she must be levitating, he rationalises, feeling the uncanny implications. The girl smiles at him, her hand extended in his direction; he knows, in that way one knows in dreams, that she wants them to dance together. So that is what they do: they dance. Around and around, levitating higher and higher above the sand with each turn, until he begs her to stop, and then falls to the sand and wakes up.

The dream has left him with an odd sensation, and he cannot go back to sleep. Everything is deep into that country-night calm when, suddenly, he hears the crackling of some sort of material, something similar to a skirt dragging over the floor. He waits, convinced that, whenever he tries to listen again, he will hear nothing. But there it is again, the sound. His eyes get more used to the darkness, and, in front of him, he sees the girl from the beach.

The feeling of unreality, of her *unreality, is so absolute and certain that he instinctively rejects the simulation, a latency glitch powerfully similar to the discontinued time with which the figure flickers in and out of his vision, advancing in his direction.*

The girl is talking, and it is possible for him to understand some of the words she is saying: hurts, fire, danger.

She continues advancing in his direction in that same way, flickering in and out of his vision, but he is certain that there are no steps on the floor, only the rustle of her long skirts combing it softly.

With trembling hands a match is lit: the same girl, no doubt; although why so certain? Could it be the simulation knowledge again? It is the same girl, or so he thinks, so he knows; but her face is disfigured, burnt.

He hears frantic voices next, all those people running below, and the smell reaches the topmost floor of the inn: the building is burning.

He looks out the window, calculates the distance, and let himself fall. He lands amorphously over his leg. The pain is horrendous, and it advances like fire through his limbs, proving to him that he is alive.

You confided in me, of all people, and I felt blessed: you were working on the perfect immersion. A child missing someone so acutely that their presence is invoked back from the ether. Not her, not the mother. But the *idea* of her, the *essence* of her, transformed into solid reality. You liked this idea exceedingly. For the first time, I felt something horrid in the notion. What do we need the simulations for? I asked. To understand, you replied. To understand what, exactly? We were so young, hardly over three hundred solar years. And yet, for them we would have been ancient. We would have suffered painfully, or perhaps our vital energy would have been suddenly flicked out, like the light of a candle. I thought those musings absurd. And then you explained. Beneath the cosmographies, deep into the forest, away in the interstellar journeys which predicated the future of our world. You had seen it in all those places, the possibility of shadows. You swore, my friend, that you *had* experienced shadows, even if this was a blasphemous thing to say.

Then you told your own story. It went like this: sitting at the high table, enjoying the feast. The robes crimson and purple, richly decorated, pointed hats and jewelled fingers dispelling the dark. You, yourself, taking your seat among the elders of the Museum. But, if you paid close attention, you'd notice their demeanour was odd, an out of place warning, like the tolling of a faraway bell in a distant town. If you looked closely, you said, you'd see they were all eating with their bare hands, bits of ancient birds and feathers and sauces smearing their costly rings, a disgusting mush shoved into their mouths with no ceremony, noisily chewed with rotten teeth. And, were you to look even more closely, you would see that the table was covered with centipedes crawling amongst the costly dishes and climbing atop the dusty wine goblets. Brown dirt, old leaves, and scraps of paper, scattered over the remains of a century-old feast, about to crumble into dust.

And then she wakes up.

Outside, a gentle rain falls. She had fallen asleep on the made-up bed, with the familiar objects scattered around her.

She lists them in her head, like she always does: the bell, the watch, the thin tin box, the faded photograph of her mother as a young student. The useless car keys of a car long gone. The little bib for a newborn baby, herself. Except. Something odd, unexpected. A door into another realm, materialising all of a sudden. Opening a whole new world of unwanted possibilities.

The bib doesn't have her name on it.

How has she not noticed this before? She has long lingered over the precious objects. Perhaps because the date of birth is correct. Only. It doesn't say Rose, it says something else.

Who is this other child? She wishes she could ask her, tell her, she wishes ...

Sometimes one desires a thing so badly, that one is capable of invoking it oneself.

The corridor is bathed in the uncertain light of dusk.

Outside the rain gushes over the walls of the house, splashing on the ramshackle conservatory attached to the main structure, leaking through the window that she can never close properly.

The shadow is, for a second, at the corner of her eye, so she turns this time, to meet her fully.

It is her mother, exactly as she remembers her in those horrid last months. The thin tall figure, the bruises on the pale skin due to her bedrridden state, the pixie haircut, the white nightgown. She is leaning against the threshold of the room.

She almost remembers something—what?—at that precise moment. It is almost there, as certainly as her mother is almost there. For she cannot fully by there. A delicate knowledge, lost to time, almost revealed by a yellowed piece of material. But, as soon as she thinks that she can grasp the thought, it flutters away, and the possible memory melts in midair, like a summer mist. It leaves nothing behind.

As if a cloud has lifted unexpectedly, revealing a place lost in time, in memory, in dreams. As if another version of reality has taken over the known place. As if in this parallel variant of her life her mother and her sadness and her illness and her defeat could somehow be explained.

The revelation, or, as you called it, your 'vision', left you breathless for more knowledge. You were trying to produce the definitive immersion at this time. It needed to be longer. That was what you said. You were trying to produce a scenario in which, perhaps, the confusion between the 'then' and the 'now', between the real and the simulation, was so great that maybe the liquid reality you had created with your technology would filter into our world. You said you were hoping to raise some dormant shadows, because the shadows, you explained, sit among us still. I had never heard you saying something so wrong, and I cringed. You carried on talking. You said that the Museum's existence was designed to help us forget this fact, that reality was altogether more complex than we credited from our orderly plane. I was shocked and confused. You blamed the Museum. Its orderly collection, you continued, gave us the false impression of a world under control, recognizable, where the categories not only give meaning but solace. You made me consider the vaporous rooms, ethereal round spaces with their little cubicles and exhibitors, and the guard in the centre ...

You make it sound like a prison, I said. And you replied that I had touched on the nerve of the matter, for some of them had been fortresses in the old days, and still were, in a manner of speaking, for they kidnapped our imagination, our capacity to feel. This was dangerous talk, edging on the punishable. I got scared: of the Museum, of you, of the horrid simulations which always left an odd taste, as of things unresolved, or as of drowning in an oily liquid.

I saw you less. A few weeks later, I visited your domed compound once more. It was hard to keep away. I could see the remnants of a party in every room. Some of your guests were still plugged to your discarded simulations. I had never before asked why all the simulations took place in the same period of the ancient era. The olden men, the fragile men, the men who died before they started living, had lived in many different eras. You explained to me it was the best documented one. Everything that could be recreated was recreated. The details available for our programming were infinite. It was easy to fool reality.

Is that what you were trying to do, fool reality? I asked about the definitive simulation you were working on. And then you explained it: the Museum had allowed snapshots, *mementos mori*, always short, which left you breathless, but also allowed you to re-enter our world. The crimson robed elders were worried that our minds could otherwise get lost inside the simulations. They needed to be like old fashioned photographs, something to look at once, to experience the antiquated feeling, and then be discarded.

Photographs? I asked. You took me to a hidden chamber. There, inside a box, you kept some unusual pieces, big, fragile, their glass lovingly preserved inside a brown leather case. You held them carefully, a question in your eyes. Negatives, you proclaimed. The first negatives from ancient times. We looked through them. They showed an ancient house. Through the light one cannot make out at the beginning the shape of the building, but then at last you distinguish a door and a tower, and suddenly the whole image reveals itself. Equally, it takes you some time to accustom your eyes to that parallel reality. You explained: when someone called William Henry Fox Talbot patented them, he called them calotypes, from the Greek *kalos*, beautiful. The camera reveals the beauty, and it is a machine designed to preserve that beauty. It is curious that, from its beginning, it was firmly believed that photography and truth were synonyms, that its main use would be to preserve antinaturally what memory was incapable of keeping. Talbot believed that it revealed more details from nature than our eyes. At the same time, a man called Daguerre was working on the same process, and his heavy plaques of bronze were known as 'mirrors with truth'. But these new techniques did not reveal the truth, you said, but rather preserved the lie. They only managed to preserve the presence of the dead in the absurdly short lives of preterite men, imprinting long-gone faces on their experience of reality. Perhaps, you theorised, the existence of these artefacts was what made them so slow in trying to lengthen life itself, because they had this kind of simulacra available. A picture, you said with finality, was nothing more than the affirmation of a shadow, of an absence.

Once outside, in your garden, among the durian plants and under the light of the two moons, you spoke again. What if the truth is inside the simulation? I was speechless. What if we are those shadows, playing at being Gods? My heart beat faster and faster. My instinct was to run away, far away. I could see it now, clearly. You were sealing your fate. The elders would offer you to the Healing. You were flying dangerously close to the flames.

After you disappeared, it took me a long time to go back to the Museum. But I thought about it often, of its willingness to accumulate, to impatiently extract order. Now I understand you better, perhaps because it is easy to see a maze from above, or because I have understood at last that here, in the Museum, we are being accounted for, labelled, domesticated. It was meant to be democratic, for everyone. To cease being one of those inaccessible fortresses of ancient times and open its doors to all. To make knowledge accessible through its collections, not to domesticate and feed it to us in little pills of contentment. Instead, it became the repository of all we extirpated from our own humanity: stolen artefacts and extinct species and dormant emotions. The basic humanity we have so effectively shed. Now, we need the Museum because we have finished off everything else. Our dying planet, not the first we've inhabited, is quickly becoming another gigantic Museum.

I miss you, and think about you often, lost in your last simulation, or so I hope. It was thought that you'd managed to create it, and to lose yourself in it. This is the legend, the myth—no one can know the truth of it.

Actually I lie. After your disappearance, the simulation was anonymously sent to me. The last one you ever made, your masterpiece. I often walk in those streets in my mind's eye, and think I see you round a corner. You are a child, but you are also you. I am one of those old men, flesh and bone, heavy step and foul breath; but I am also me. Inside the simulation, we are together, although we should not be. I could swear the air smells of you sometimes.

You know it, for you are one of them. There are those in your profession who swear that the best among you are not those who know how to apply conservation techniques, but rather those who know how to destroy. Weeding, it is called. You cannot think of anything more ridiculous. You recall Voltaire: To the dead we owe only the truth. You cannot get to the truth by destroying.

The snowdrift has covered the town, and people do not know how to act. They crash against one another, walk up and down with difficulty, take refuge in improvised spaces. Everyone experiences the same lethargic state of the provisional, which forces us to abandon our assigned paths and rehearse other possible existences.

You are now in the middle of the archive. Silence swallows it all. The possibility of the smallest indication of life is entirely gone before the calm that accompanies the unexpected falling of the snow. You are filling the kettle when, suddenly, you experience something impossible but exact: the presence of your little brother in the next room, the one that doubles as sitting room and small office.

A pain in your stomach serves as announcement of the terror that, you logically suppose, must accompany a situation of this kind. You can hear him climbing on the old chair; it's impossible to know why you're certain that it is him, him. You walk slowly into the room. There is no one, nothing unusual—on future occassions the presence would manifest in many different ways. The chair holds the form of a body, but it could be yours, and you have just never noticed it before. You put your hand on the place, expecting ... warmth? That is absurd. Your adoptive brother is dead, after all. Pale, shadows under his eyes, cold to the touch. You walk distractedly to the window and you see the first unusual thing: a small child crossing the quad. In the dusk it is difficult to discern, but you could swear that he is not wearing shoes, a hat, or a coat despite the weather. He does not seem to leave prints in the recently fallen snow, as if he is flying instead of running.

The charm is broken. Your conventual life had managed to keep him at bay, although from time to time his shadow was summoned each dusk. But now all that is gone, and you are alone, again.

Later, in that uncertain moment between wakefulness and sleep, you come to understand that Benjamin is standing at the end of your room. You don't need to look there to know. Now you know why his asthmatic breathing, hardly recalled the night before, is now a certain memory slowly revealed, as if you were looking at a negative. You feel so much terror that you are sure you levitate a few centimetres off the mattress.

Since then, he comes every night. Lying on your bed, it is difficult to move, to make a decision as simple as to get up and get on with the day, which now passes in crescent horror at the approaching evening. Sometimes you wake from a useless and light drowse, incapable of moving. But you are not able to sleep again, knowing that he is there. You are paralysed on these occasions, your throat dry. Eventually, it is the need for a smoke that brings about the miracle, and you abandon your rooms dishevelled, the college porters already looking for you, so out of character is it for you to go against the established order of things.

You stay then, paralysed, immobile. At the end of the quad you need to cross, impossibly filled at this early hour by hordes of tourists who are desecrating the white, you see him again, a small, greyish boy, dirty and not clad for the weather, moving among the group of people who are leaving the quad in an orderly line. Though they do not seem to see him, they go around him, in a strange dance, which makes you think that relationships between the living and the dead are impossible, antinatural, that their worlds are one over the other without ever touching, like oil and water. Benjamin turns around and walks resolutely to the exit. This gets you moving: you have never seen him outside of the college. You run to the main entrance, now filled with people, and start pulling all the tourists away one by one, shouting apologies to the air, to none of those people in particular.

I open my eyes, myself again. As always, experiencing the ancient world leaves an unpleasant taste. But I feel closer to you, my friend. It's as though you were here once more. I have resolved to work at the Museum. It is not possible to talk about you, you have become one more shadow, a forbidden thing. An artifact from the past we have discarded. You specialised in shadows, and now there is no one to take your place. I am scared we are forgetting how to experience this emotion, how we fear ... Nothing. The elders who ask me questions do not seem surprised at my offer. They readily agree. I am shown into an apartment of round chambers where I am to conduct my research, and left there.

This time of year is particularly difficult. A never-ending spring, infinitely cruel in its vastness. But eventually it will burn itself out, and the planets will realign once more. The flames of Sun-003 will almost reach the cristal domes and white turrets. The elders work fast to finish the calculations. The Healing approaches.

On the day itself, a procession of crimson robes will cross the citadel at twilight, and, on the mantelpiece, a clock will tick away somebody's last breath with stubborn persistence. One, two, three. Soon, it will be time. The procession is quietly approaching.

I think of you, of those bells ringing the quarters, and me knowing, with a frightful certainty, that you did not disappear into a simulation. This sudden certainty, useless at the time it has chosen to reveal itself, upsets me more than I can explain.

When the old men arrive, I will go with them, smiling. I have lived enough, in any case, and the Healing must be done. Something else needs to be extirpated, annihilated, vanished, made extinct from this world, for our sake, for all our sakes—this destruction is our only credo, the only way we know how to survive. And soon none of us will be able to feel it, or to remember it ever existed. And so I will go, smiling. Or perhaps in that former emotion, fear. Will I remember how to feel it, after all?

M's Awfully Big Adventure

> *La muerte es de los otros.*
> Death belongs to others.
>
> —Homero Aridjis

Winona Ryder looks at me, sceptically. She stops checking my documentation, and one hand pauses in mid-air, still holding a few sheets of paper; the thumb of her other hand is at her lips—she's about to lick it, so as to speed up the paper-shuffling process. I feel like I should explain myself, and I remember similar scenes in doctors' consulting rooms—*Pull yourself together woman, it's not that bad*—as I tried to explain a very specific ache, a problem. Using all the arguments at my disposal just to be taken seriously.

'It's not possible,' is all she says. I remember hundreds of similar scenes, this time in offices, trying to sweet-talk some drone with the power to bring an important piece of business home successfully, or else cancel it altogether. In these, my face would get stuck in a psychotic grin as I tried to convince the jobsworth that all my documentation was present and correct, or at least submitted by the guillotine cut-off date.

Automatically, my face slips into that same psychotic grin.

The result is not positive.

'Why are you laughing? You think this cockup is funny?'

Winona Ryder is now even more serious, if that were possible. I wipe the smile from my face in a millisecond.

I'm not really sure where I am. The office is small, and only lit by the yellowish light of a single reading lamp. The smoke from Winona's cigarette makes it look a bit like something out of a cop movie. I can't remember how I got here, how I got in. I can't see any doors.

'Let's see if I can get this straight,' Winona starts again, her patience almost palpable. She picks up her cigarette and takes another drag while she looks through the paperwork once more. 'So, you left your place of work ... The bookshop?'

'Library,' I correct to the air.

'Okay, okay ... Right. So, you left at your usual time.' She looks at me, trying to get me to confirm her accusation.

'Yes, that's right,' I say, wanting to show my willingness to collaborate.

'Good. So, you went down the street from this ... mmm ... *library* ... until you reached the main boulevard, and then you went round the corner and headed towards Miralles Street.'

'That's right.'

'Good. Good.' Another drag on the cigarette. Winona looks through some more forms. 'And then here it says, quite clearly, that you "got hit by a tram" when you tried to cross the street.'

'That's correct, yes.'

The look that Winona gives me is tremendous. It's meant to show me that she's been right from the very beginning of our interview, a point which I no longer remember and which now seems neither very long ago nor very recent, but which could be hours away. Weeks, centuries. I clear my throat.

'But you have to bear in mind that it only brushed me.'

'It knocked you over, that's what it says here in black and white,' Winona says, the tip of her finger prodding insistently into the papers. If she's not careful she'll make a hole in them, first the papers, and then the table. I can't understand what's going on. Yes, alright, I did get hit by the tram, but I got up again right away, and then got onto the pavement, and looked through the window of the second-hand shop, like I always do when I'm walking home, just to check if they've got something in about my favourite vintage TV serialisation. I got up by myself, without anyone helping me. But the point is to explain it to Winona so that she understands what I'm saying. I got up by myself, it was just a bruise. I carried on walking home. How the hell can I make her understand me?

I'm a nothing in this office, a complete nobody. But this isn't a new situation for me. I often find myself offering explanations to complete strangers, caught up in tangled situations because of some misunderstanding or other. Like when my work colleague accused me of stealing her sandwich from the shared office fridge. I know that I looked guilty, that there was a telltale egg-stain on my shirt, but it really wasn't me who stole the sandwich, and the stain came from the day before. Unbelievably (I suppose that's part of the problem) I'd had to put a dirty shirt on that morning because I hadn't had time to put a wash in over the weekend. I had spent two whole days without leaving my room, suffering from a horrible anxiety attack, caused specifically by the fact that I had too many things to do and didn't know where to start, and one of these things was, of course, putting a wash in. But who on earth would believe so many coincidences, piled up one on top of another?

And now I'm in a similar situation, with the aggravating factor that Winona has it in her power to allow me to go home, or else to make me stay where I am for all eternity. Winona told me that this was the Afterlife as soon as I entered her office, just like that, no attempt to soften the blow, and showed me where I needed to sign to confirm my recent decease. With reflexes that impressed even me, I refused to sign anything. But I was finding it very hard to convince Winona, get her to believe that I wasn't dead. Far from it.

Alright, it's true that I was hurrying as I left the library. There was a hint, a rumour, that they were going to release a new episode of my favourite vintage TV serialisation on the web. I had spent most of the day—in between cataloguing book after book and helping people fill in reader-card request forms and stamping return dates on slips—glued to my splitmirror, hiding among the shelves and trying to follow the gossip on the forums. It was a very old series, one that I only started watching because of my parents. They had met at a so-called 'convention', a kind of vast shindig where fans meet the creators of these fictions, and there were talks, and you could buy guidebooks and t-shirts with your favourite characters, and mugs with the logo on them, and in general everything to do with fictional things. There's nothing like that now, of course, and the idea of locking yourself away in a hotel with hundreds of strangers in order to share an obsession seems somehow both barbaric and old-fashioned. I do have one of the coffee mugs at home, inherited from my parents. It is one of my dearest possessions. The family legend is that my parents saw the whole series, pilot to finale, while my mother was pregnant with me. That, at least, took persistence. It was a series that had started in the middle of the last century, and which had run for three decades, more or less, with six to ten episodes per year. And then it took a long break, before being revived at the beginning of the twenty-first century. Then it had paused again for several decades, and was then brought back as an internet-only serialisation, produced (one suspected) by a hard-core group of fans. They had recently announced a competition to write a new episode, and of course I put myself forward. I try to write when I can, outside my shifts at the library: mostly stories that are half sci-fi, half horror, or ghost stories. I don't write according to any particular genre: I like to experiment and mix things up. That makes things difficult, especially when it comes to convincing someone to actually publish them.

The fictional TV serialisation was not my chief obsession. Ever since I was a little girl, my first main interest—my first crush—had been the movies of an American director, who had worked towards the end of the twentieth century, some of whose films survived. Most of them were in colour, but a very few were in black and white, which was very odd indeed: only films from the prehistory of cinema had been filmed in those strange greyish tones, because back then they hadn't worked out how to get normal colour stuck to the rolls of ancient film they used. And this director, who had been very famous, and won lots of prizes, and made a whole bunch of films, was now practically forgotten. People remembered his favourite star much more: it was none other than Winona Ryder herself. Winona's career had passed and surpassed that of the director, and she became truly famous when she started to take on roles in a number of TV serialisations, the kind that played with the narrative codes that the audience knew all too well, forming a kind of witty hash, recycling the plots of kids' shows from the previous century, shows about paranormal investigations, and even soap-operatic cop shows. The Winona who appeared in those was a middle-aged woman, a mother courage type, a professional loser, poking fun at her own career via her choice of roles, poking fun at her own life, making ever more head-spinningly self-referential connections between reality and fiction—that's what my parents and their generation seemed to like, all those cultural consumers who came of age a generation or two before mine. For me, my favourite Winona was quite another: the young girl with the long blonde hair who fell in love with a boy with knives for hands, like a kind of primitive cybernetic adaptation; or else—yes, I liked this one even more—the girl whose parents didn't understand her, who had the strange power of being able to see the recent dead, which got her into ever more serious trouble ... Although the rapturous happy ending to the film shows that there is always a chance of compromise, cohabitation between two worlds. That Winona was my first serious crush.

The Winona in front of me now is a strange mixture of my memories of movies and TV serialisations. She's decked out in the dark designer clothes that the psychic teenager wore—her name in that particular movie was Lydia, by the way—but she looks like an old woman, just as she did in the last serialisation she starred in, a TV fiction from my own childhood where Winona took the role of Tiffani, a retired librarian who crisscrossed some indeterminate country (probably the former United States of America; even more probably filmed in Canada), killing monsters and preventing an invasion by demons and fallen angels; you know the kind of thing: a hodgepodge of loads of the series that had come before, with different narrative twists that we've all seen hundreds of times.

The Winona in front of me now, the old woman dressed as a teenage Goth, chain-smokes and insists on denying my version of events. I can't help but notice how odd it is for her and no one else to be here, right here and now, and I suddenly have an idea: maybe I'm asleep? Did I faint? Am I in some kind of coma?

'Just a second,' I start. It's me who now needs to put what happened into some kind of order. Winona's presence here is ... too much of a coincidence, even for me. I have an idea, formulate a question: 'So, just so we get things straight. Who did you say you were, exactly?'

Winona is not happy, neither with my tone nor the question itself. She purses her lips, lifts her neck as much as her eighty-year-old body will permit, and replies, with all the disdain she can muster:

'Young lady, for the umpteenth time, I am your assigned social assistant in the Afterlife, and my job is to deal with everything connected with ...'

'Like in the Tim Burton movie?' I blurt out. I can't help myself. Winona doesn't seem at all happy with the interruption.

'Movie? What movie?' she says indignantly.

'You're not telling me it's not too much of a coincidence ...'

'What are you talking about?'

'Just that. You tell me I'm dead, and then the Afterlife is just like a Tim Burton movie!' I'm getting into the swing of things. I feel very happy with my deduction. Of course, I must be imagining it all, or else I *really* am in a coma. The question is how to prove it.

'*Teen* Burton? Who the hell is *Teen* Burton?' Winona is trying to kill me with her glare. I'm not going to let myself be stared down, not now I've come this far, so I carry on:

'Now you're going to get out the *Handbook for the Recently Deceased* and tell me to read it carefully ...' I laugh-out-lout. But Winona doesn't seem to think this is at all funny. She says nothing, her mouth stretched out in a thin line, but simply gets up and goes over to a supply cupboard. Then she throws a heavy hardback book towards me. Unbelievably, the *Handbook for the Recently Deceased* slams down on the table.

Let's go through this again. I crossed Miralles Street, which, okay, I admit I may have done quickly and without looking. Something astounding had happened, one of those coincidences that seems to happen to me more often than to other people, but which then take a lot of time and energy to explain. So: it was a number of years since my obsession for the films of that director had been replaced by my new obsession for the TV serialisation about the two-hearts time-traveller, and, as I said, I was hurrying home in the hope of there being a new episode available. What happened was that I noticed something in the window of the second-hand shop, where I always used to stop on the way home. It was a kind of long, black-and-white striped tube, that made me think immediately about some of the creatures that figured in the old director's grand-guignol aesthetics. I couldn't believe it! I craned my neck: I couldn't see if it was a doll or whatever it was, but that black and white stripy worm was ever so very familiar, and brought back happy memories of moments from my childhood, hiding under the duvet and watching old films on my splitmirror. Now I could see it better: it was a long plush worm, ending in a face that was all mouth, a huge mouth open and full of sharp teeth, with two little eyes above it. Yes, now I could see it more clearly. The problem is that in order to see it more clearly I had walked towards the shop without looking where I was going, and now I was in the middle of the street, standing on the tracks that the silent and treacherous tram was duty-bound to follow.

It really wasn't a very hard blow. It hit me on the side, on my hip, and knocked me to the ground. But I got up straight away. Everything was fine. Nothing to see here. I kept my eyes on the shop window and walked ever closer, as close as possible. In the centre of the display, a selection of books about the director, the soft toy that I had seen from the other side of the street, and in the clear protective case something amazing: a so-called 'd-v-d', or 'digital-versatile-disc', that's what they're called; an authentic, a relic, an extremely valuable antique that came from who knows where and cost who knows what, and which was, just to rub it in, a copy of the very same film in which Winona played the part of Lydia, and where the snake-like monsters that I saw now in front of me in soft-toy form had appeared for the very first time.

I was so shocked to see the 'd-v-d' there, in front of me, that I didn't realize what I was doing. And what I was doing was something that I couldn't really have explained in any case: suddenly I saw myself holding the very same 'd-v-d'. I had it in my hand. I had taken it out of the shop window and was holding it up to my face. I was scared once I realized what I had done, and so, before any alarm went off, I put it back in its place and headed off quickly back towards my house. I tried not to think, I realise now; I tried to force out of my head all kinds of absurd questions, such as how I had even managed to touch it, let alone take it out of the shop window. My hand would have needed to go through the glass, and then through the protective bubble that contained the valuable object. How the hell had my hand gone through the glass? I had no idea. It must have been that my excitement at seeing a 'digital-versatile-disc' for the first time in my life must have unleashed some kind of magic or special power, similar to the supernatural strength mothers are said to obtain when they see their offspring caught under the wheels of a truck. Or something like that, anyway.

I've written a lot of ghost stories in my life. Each one worse than the one that came before. Ghost stories have certain predetermined characteristics:

🪶 They tend to be sad, melancholy. That's understandable, given that they are about absences, someone or something that is missing.

🪶 They tend to be 'odd', but with a kind of oddness that distorts the everyday, especially in domestic settings.

🪶 They've got more atmosphere than plot to them, and more descriptions than dialogue.

🪶 They tend to take place in specific environments: a haunted house, a dark forest, a grotesque moorland, an abandoned spaceship, an alternate reality that only looks very slightly like our own.

🪶 It's always raining in ghost stories, and the thunder is crashing and the lightning flashes.

🪶 The most unexpected plot twists often take place in the last line. Some of my favourites are *'But you couldn't have seen him ... he died ten years ago!'*, or else the incomparable *'It turns out the ghost ... is you!'*

And what if I am asleep now, or in a coma, and I'm imagining everything? Well, if I analyse what's happening, my current situation has nothing in common with what I've just set out. Given that I like ghost stories, wouldn't it be logical, or at least likely, that my mind would have decided to construct a narrative that followed those particular patterns? On the other hand, if I'm not imagining it all, then how is it possible that the bloody Afterlife ends up modelled on ...? Hang on a second. All I've seen so far is Winona's office. I should try to remember something about how I got here, what happened on the way home, and then on the way from home to this place.

Nothing, nothing at all. Nothing happened, or rather I forgot about anything that had happened, because I couldn't remember the first thing about walking along Miralles Street to get to my house, my little flat on the dead-end road that abuts onto Miralles Street itself. I cut straight from the scene where I'm running away from the second-hand shop at full tilt into one where I'm already at home, straight away, like in one of those old and badly-edited movies. What the hell ...?

I have to admit, even if only to myself, that this doesn't look good.

Anyway. Once I was back home I did what I always do: made myself a strong cup of tea, microwaved a ready meal—chicken curry—and then straight to the computer, right onto the digital channel where, if I'm lucky, I'll meet with my favourite time-traveller.

Normally, when an episode is about to drop, a huge clock is counting down on the channel's home page. For the time being there was nothing, or rather there was a completely black screen and nothing else. I opened the Word document with the story I had been writing for the last couple of weeks, and started to read what I'd got so far while I ate my curry and drank my tea ...

Hang on a second. Oh. I am not at all sure that I ate the curry. I have no memory of having done so, and I don't remember the flavour or anything at all. What does chicken curry taste like? And what about tea?

The telephone rang: I remember that very well. Not my split, but a very old rotary telephone that must have come from the second-hand shop, that I didn't remember having plugged in, or even buying. Anyway, I got up as soon as it rang and went, mechanically, straight over to where it lived, on a little table in the hallway; I picked up the handset and put it straight to my ear:

'Yes?' I spoke into the ether.

'Good morning, I'm sorry to bother you.' Good morning? It must be late at night already. 'I was wondering if you'd got the contract, and if you've had a chance to look it over.'

'The contract? Which contract?'

'The contract for the sale of the apartment, of course. This is Felix, from Lucian Fox.'

Nothing that this gentleman on the other end of the phone line said made any sense.

'I'm sorry, I think you must have the wrong number.'

'Excuse me?'

'You dialled the wrong number.'

Papers rustling on the other end of the line; he's checking something.

'Are you sure?' Sometimes male self-confidence really drives me up the wall. How could I not be sure? My flat was not for sale. 'Isn't this number four Acacia Lane, flat 2E?' Felix from Lucian Fox insisted.

I didn't believe it. That was my address. I was a bit befogged, and looked out of the window, as though the outside world would have an answer to such a large problem. I was shocked to see that it was light outside, that it probably was morning. How long had I dropped off for in front of the computer?

'There must be some mistake,' I said. 'My flat is not for sale.' I thought that the best thing I could do would be to clear things up straight away. But now there was no sound from the other end of the line. 'Hello? Are you still there?'

I noticed then a sort of square shadow that covered half of the window. I hung up and went to investigate: you couldn't make it out all that well from inside, but yes, it seemed like it really was a FOR SALE sign.

'What the hell ...?'

Indignantly I headed off to the door to my flat, wanting to see the sign in more detail from the street. What time was it? Was I going to be late to work? It was very strange, but I looked around and couldn't see a clock anywhere. My splitmirror was nowhere to be found either.

I opened the door resolutely, grabbing my raincoat off the hook as I left. I was just putting it on when ...

I stopped myself just in time. One more step and I would have fallen into the void. There was nothing past my front door, just an abyss that seemed to go on for ever.

'So, now you know. You need to sign in triplicate. If you don't, then you won't be able to go back home and have a normal afterlife.'

'Normal? What do you mean, normal? I'm dead! For God's sake!'

'Come on, don't get like that ... It's possible to live a full and interesting life, even if you are dead. Let's think about it. What did you do when you were alive?'

'I'm a ... I was a librarian.' I see her face turn slightly sour.

'Yeah. Hmm, that's tricky. No. No, people here don't read very much. Didn't you do anything else?'

'I liked to write stories.'

She perks up.

'Perfect! You'll have all the time in the world to write; you won't have to keep an eye on the clock. You'll never get tired, you won't need to eat; you certainly won't have to go and waste half your time in some tedious job.'

'But ... Didn't you say that people don't read much here?'

'Yes, that's true ... Nobody reads at all, but there are a lot of writers. Lift up a stone and hundreds of them come crawling out. Writers, poets, hah!' Winona laughs terrifyingly, only breaking off to have a coughing fit. 'Look, you go and write, spend time doing what you like doing. Then, when the time is right, we'll tell you where you can send your little stories.'

'You mean ... they'll be published?'

'Mmmhmm.'

'There are publishers ... here?'

'Yes, but ... Well, it's better if you know someone, if you've got a friend in the right places ... Or you could always be on the dead telly, that shifts a lot of copies.'

Great, what a joke. The publishing scene in the Afterlife seems to have learnt its tricks from the world above.

'What do you mean, the dead telly?'

'It's a channel they show down here ... Some people have fun making little programmes, and then there's the Afterlife News and things like that ... Soap operas, even.'

'Soap operas ...' I repeat. I've just had a wonderful idea. 'Is there anything about time-travellers?'

I never got round to asking my social assistant why she looked so much like Winona, but I have my little theories. I suppose it must be that when you get here they try to cheer you up by offering you a friendly face, someone who makes you think about the happier bits of your life. Anyway, now I have all the time in the world to do what I've always wanted to do, and I'm more or less happy. To begin with it took a bit of effort, I won't deny it, but now it's obvious. Of course, it turns out the ghost ... is me.

II

II

Voyage to the White Sea

a weary man rows against the wind ...
—Anglo-Saxon poem

1. Upon ascertaining that the sea extends as far North as we can imagine possible, we decided to find its end. A weary man is said to row against the wind; but we are no men. And women row with hope, with wonder. We sought the end as we sought truth. A safe passage. Further lands for our Queen to trade with and conquer. Fantastical beasts. These all proved dreams. And what is an ending but a dream? And so into the dream we wandered.

We thought our task simple: it was not.

What we didn't expect was the White Sea.

We followed the land North until it turned abruptly towards the East. It was the time to change course, to skirt the coast, to follow the well-trodden path, into the land of the Norwegians, into the land of the Swedes, Halogaland, Sciringesheal, the trading-town where a woman could sail in as little as thirty dawns if she happened upon favourable wind. We left the Lapps behind us, to the South of Sciringesheal, where a very great sea starts and extends up; it is broader than any woman can see across. Once you come to the other side, you reach Hedeby, the Danish enclave which stands between Wends and Angles; Jutland opposite.

But our course was other; our course took us into the unknown, the unimaginable: hundreds upon hundreds of miles of sea and only sea.

ii. We changed course, away from the embrace of known lands, every stroke taking us further from home. Whale-hunters venture no more than three dawns out. We decided to travel a fourth dawn into the open sea, then a fifth, then a sixth. On the sixth night, that was the first time we saw them, the blue-white light, with its many constellations dancing around: the fox, the raven, the wheel, and that other we could not place, but that looked like a burial-child, bent upon himself in sacrifice, forever holding his legs, forever embracing his mortality.

The dogs complained in their cages, watching the worrying sky. The sky was tired, the land was tired, the sea was tired, tired of the promise of an ending that never came. Further North we went, and further North we kept going; North, always North, North eternally;

until everything on view was blue, and purple, and even green; and that shiny sickly white.

iii. Then it happened that we came upon it: the White Sea.

iv. At the beginning of our travels, there had been other boats keeping us company, the small boats of wood and skin preferred by our fisherwomen, the oar-propelled vessels, the ring prow, the curve-neck wood, sea-goers, wave-traversers, with their fierce, valiant she-warriors. Now, we had been alone for many a dawn. We missed their company over the dark waters, the collective joy of a stretch of blue sky further beyond, begging to be chased, inciting us beyond the black clouds.

We stopped seeing animals entirely, except for a whale. It was much smaller than others we had encountered: seven ells long, when normally they are forty-seven.

There was nothing on view now: no land, no reindeer, no cattle, no sheep, no horses. No whales, no seals, no animal skins, or bird feathers. No vessels. No she-warriors.

v. Our vessel, the traveller, was designed by you, my Queen. A fast beast, sixty mighty oars, twice as long as the Danish ashwoods and swifter, steadier, much taller; and built in its own shape, neither the Frisian nor the Danish. If the Viking ships were made to bring terror, and destruction, and death, our mighty beast was conceived by your bright mind to vanish darkness, to understand the unknown. But we were alone now, and the White Sea was cruel.

In our desire to travel further than anyone else we had forgotten that we could end up becoming that dread thing, a burial ship, a funeral ship, a ship pushed into the waters, nobly equipped with treasure, and wargear, helmets, shields, armour; set alight or not; the ashes blowing up and becoming a new constellation perhaps; and us, bent figures, holding our legs, unwilling sacrifices lying next to our swords, our attempts at maps, our feeble prayers.

As the wind stopped, the ship stopped; we were forced to stay put, bathed in that strange bluish light, the White Sea a mockery that confounded us: some saw their homes, heard their men calling. The visions were comforting, but ten times crueller when they revealed themselves as mere shadows. Sleep came, and we fell down a black well; and visions became dreams, of lands further beyond, of large standing precious stones, the light upon them, sending rainbows back into the ether. And when we woke we found ourselves still in that dream, as if we had never left it, as if now it was where we lived.

Could it be a dream? We reflected: by then the land itself had become a capricious idea. After appearing and disappearing for many a dawn, mocking us, it had now vanished entirely; and its promise, drowsed in green, and purple, and blue clouds, was a thing to behold, but nonetheless imagined, unreal. Some women cried:

they feared that the land would forever be gone, not understanding that it was already gone, that the bright-coloured lands were no less a mirage. They feared that we would be trapped forever on the white waters, failing to see that we were already trapped.

This went on for four more dawns; or what we imagined were dawns. The White Light of the White Sea meant there were no more sunsets, the whole stretch of eternity bending itself over the White Time. We had stopped knowing when was dawn, when was sunset. We were blinded to the passage of time, days and nights one same, hellish White stretch, out onto the White Sea.

vi. The constellations opened then, a window into the unknown.

And the boat danced wildly: despite the lack of wind, soaring waves were playing with us mercilessly. We clutched the boat as if our lives depended on it. We could not see land, apart from those wrong, shady versions of home that were only temptation; but now we could not even see the sky, it had become a distant dream itself. There were only blue lights, and purple, and green, crossing it like thunder; and the White Sea below us, soaring like a mountain in the gigantic waves.

vii. Soon, it was only the White. The ship soared onto the sky.

There was a window there; and through it we could see settlements made of the same-coloured lights, with winged creatures gliding above them; fantastical animals prancing among the greenery, grey and green and gigantic. I wanted to turn back, but there was no wind to help us, no wind, *no wind, alas!*

We were floating towards the opening between the clouds.

Now, the White Sea was visible below us, the only thing, neverending.

And what is the White?

It's nothing and it's everything. Hated and beloved. The only thing that connected us home, and we were leaving it behind.

As we soared up, only to come down with fury, any second threatening to be the last, I saw some of my brave women jump into the White. Some others were pulling their hair, scratching at their eyes. The dogs were wailing madly now, ferociously biting their cages, longing to be free. They were wailing at the dawn and at the blue-purple-greenish light, and at all the wrong stars that confounded us. As I saw the women go over the boat, I cried for the first time.

There was no sea below us, not even the White, as we soared above the clouds, joining them.

There was no vessel either, no mighty beast, as our minds now travelled freely. No wood, no leather, no whalebone.

viii. This transitory life. This collection of skin and bones. This beginning and this end.

It will happen to you as well, noble warrior. Death comes for us all.

Now you exist in your fullness; but this is a mirage, as certain as the White Sea. Soon it will pass: no more hunger, no more thirst, no more pain, no more wonder.

And you will ask: where has the young woman gone? Where the treasure-giver? Where the tables upon which the feast was laid? Where are the horses? Oh, mighty cup of joy! Oh, blessed feast! Time passes, darkness overcomes us, storms lashes, snow falls over us all, winter reaps, shadows grow, hailstorms blind. You are transient. The land is transient. The sea is transient. The only thing that remains is the White. For we are all pilgrims, ploughing on, exiled from the eternal place.

The stormed calmed down, and the White Sea finally swallowed us.

Oh, what wonders will we encounter now?

Ready or Not

> *Omnia mutantur nos et mutamur in illis.*
> All things change and we must change with them.
> —Unknown

I.

There is a birch tree at the edge of the back garden, that bends over the next-door neighbour's house on the other side. It looks as if it is trying to get as far away as possible. Miraculously, in a north-facing suburban garden, it happens to be a fairly majestic tree. She knows the birch tree protects children; she just doesn't know why she has this knowledge, where it comes from. A Russian novel, probably.

The vet had presented her with three options. To burn the cat and give her back the ashes. To burn the cat and disappear the ashes, so she wouldn't have to see anything, or deal with anything. Or, the third option, to give back the cat to take home with her, so she could bury him in her garden. This option had sounded wrong to her, unclean. But then she saw the prices on the piece of paper she had to sign to allow them to euthanize him, and meekly said that she would take him with her. And here she was, under the birch tree, digging again at the same little spot. I could put it where I put the other thing three months ago, she thought, for the last thing she had wanted to do was to tell Julian about it, and flushing it down the toilet had seemed to her barbaric. So she said nothing, took some paracetamol for the pain, excused the whole thing as strong PMS and then a heavy month, and brought it back there. The thought that her beloved kitty Baptiste would now keep it company was comforting.

The only thought now was, would the rats dig him up? There was nothing else she could do, better not to think about it.

There she was again. Alison was sure: her neighbour was on the other side of the garden fence. The fence was high, and she could not see her. But she knew, she could sense the old woman walking around the garden, nipping here, nipping there, removing a sneaky bud, crouching down to kill a weed. Now and again a twig snapped under her feet, grass waved at her passing, a coal tit would fly out to make way for her. The old woman had that quality, of being there, of disappearing. Alison had not heard her leave the house. As she moved the energy changed, until she knew that the woman was standing against the fence again, staring into the vine-rotten wood, right in front of Alison and her tree.

Ready or not, here I come.

Where was Julian? Why had he left her alone?

The old woman had never talked much to them, or at all to Alison. She had spoken to Julian on a few occasions about issues connected to their respective gardens, the need for him to trim it a bit here and there. As far as Alison remembered, the old woman had never exchanged a word with her, like those ladies who hardly acknowledged her, did not include her in the conversations.

It was Julian who used to say that she was going to get them. This was his particular joke. He would draw a picture for Alison's benefit, their elderly neighbour in front of a cauldron, a ladle moving of its own accord. Some familiar lurking nearby, making itself useful. A toad, perhaps. Or a bird. They knew she had no cats, that she despised cats.

Alison could not tell half the time if he was being serious or joking. He sometimes used jokes to discuss painful, traumatic issues, or to attack her, and other times jokes were simply jokes. This was how they interacted, second-guessing each other. Then the thing with the cats happened.

Some neighbours from the street got kittens. It happened like this: they had small children and wanted to find something to keep them entertained during the long periods of confinement. These neighbours lived in one of the prettiest Victorian cottages, an immaculate academic dwelling. They had never been invited inside, but at some point the neighbours had put their house on the market, and Julian looked at the pictures online and had admired, jealously, their collection of books. As if they themselves did not have enough books, occupying every single available wall, the whole of the spare bedroom filled with boxes, more boxes in the garage, modular bookshelves everywhere. The neighbour was a Shakespeare scholar, and he gave the cats pretty Shakespearean names. They were beautiful cats, black with white paws and bellies, the kind that everyone remembers from children's stories. Their neighbours let them out of the house, that was their mistake. And they hunted. People started finding dead birds, unwanted offerings at their front doors.

Why did they do nothing to protect them? Julian claimed not to be at all surprised when one of the cats appeared in the apple tree that stood in the little patch of green right in front of the old woman's house, dead with his guts spilling out. The other one was never seen again.

'She got them at last!' was all he said, an odd, manic smile dancing on his face. Alison thought that it was the first time she has seen him look scared of being right. Being right was important for Julian.

It was the violence that got Alison. If it really had been the old lady, why do it like that? She could have poisoned them, for instance, but instead she chose to do something unspeakable. It broke the street, whatever community had been built up in its makeshift way. Until then, neighbours had congregated in their doorsteps with mugs of tea and coffee on Sunday mornings, just to keep a check on who was still alive behind their doors. Now, all this stopped abruptly. There was a silent acknowledgement that something else was going on, something that had been easier to ignore in the days when everyone went about their business, had meetings to attend, jobs to perform, shopping to do. Now, there was nowhere to go, and the little street was all their world. And that world was smaller somehow.

The academic neighbours with the immaculate book-lined house moved out soon after.

2.

One thing she missed was *that* noise, the *clack clack clack* of Baptiste's little paws on the wooden floor. But that was all. An advantage of Julian's unexpected desertion was that the house without him was silent. She had no idea where he was, or what he might be doing. It was comforting. For too long she had been secretary, organiser, maid, and everything else in between. Without Julian prancing around, she could go out into the garden, kept secluded by the overgrown sumac, walk to the birch tree, and have a sneaky cigarette—he would certainly not approve. Later on, she could sit in front of the computer and check the early twentieth-century Japanese edition of *Alice* that was going, incredibly cheap, to the highest bidder. It was a little life of sorts, only her, the acrid cigarette, the pacing up and down to the tree.

The birch tree. She knew she would have to do something about it, plant some bulbs, perhaps in the spring. The turned earth looked terrible, brought horrid thoughts. The smell was much more powerful than she had expected. She put out the cigarette and walked the stone path back to the conservatory door, all the time wondering if her neighbour was following her progress on the other side of the fence. So quiet, so still ... But a stillness that had some dense purpose within it. What purpose, exactly? The unanswered question. Alison opened the door, went back inside, closed the door; only then she noticed it, her heart quietly racing inside her ribcage.

The thing is, the neighbour's dead cat had hit them hard, for back then Baptiste was still alive. Baptiste, their fat slow house cat, who had thankfully never been let out. Whenever Alison looked from her bedroom window, Baptiste would come and sit on the windowsill and purr, looking to the outer world. Alison knew what he wanted, for her to open the window so he could smell the outside. She was wary of doing this, as once, in the old neighbourhood, he had fallen asleep on the windowsill, and dropped three storeys from their rented apartment. She had another reason not to want to open the window. She was scared of letting something else in. The cat was now following, with his old, watery eyes, the progress of some birds strutting around the messy garden.

And there she was. Very straight, unmoving. From her vantage point, Alison glimpsed a faded pink fleece through the green and the branches. What was she doing? That was the first time she had seen her like this, staring at the fence without moving, like a child who had been punished. There was some oddness in her position. The old lady was shorter than her, with a stocky upper body and short legs, strong and lean arms for her age. She had hardly any neck, and her head was too big for her body. She reminded Alison of a puppet, the way she stood. Her head was covered by a mane of white hair that she cut over her shoulder and in a lopsided fringe, and never put up. It was difficult to explain why that big round head with no neck made her so scary. Dusk fell, the twin suburban gardens folding themselves into evening hibernation. Why was she there? What was she doing? It looked as if she was about to turn, and go and search for someone hiding.

Ready or not.

Slowly, slowly, the old woman started turning in her direction, until she was staring at them, Alison and Baptiste. Alison had waved at the woman through her fear; those were the earlier days, the days when she still thought her neighbours and co-workers would include her despite looking so decidedly *not-from-these-parts*. The old woman did not react. She just continued looking in her direction, white hair quite unruly, black eyes dark beyond understanding. It was probably the distance, but they looked completely black, two dead pebbles. The next few days, Alison would have nightmares about them.

Alison's stomach had contracted, and she walked backwards in fear, painfully hitting her calves on the bed. She could still see her from the bedroom window. Suddenly, with a jerking movement, the woman turned around and started furiously working, pruning and cutting and dragging things in a wheelbarrow, the very image of industry, that little old lady, with white hair, no neck, and a round and thick head, too big for her diminutive body, that old lady strong beyond her years. The image was suburban, normal. Except it was not.

There is no one else doing this. The street is deserted. Everyone else is inside their homes, watching television, preparing themselves for another long weekend with nowhere to go. There is no one else because all the other gardens are showing the desolation of winter; that is, except *her* garden. A garden suspended in time, a somehow not-quite-winter garden. An impossible, unnatural oddity, pruning, digging, planting, when everybody else's strip of grass is brown and muddy and dead, and will remain so for months to come. How to explain the impossible? she wonders, for a fragment of a second. Then, it all goes up like smoke, and she forgets. How easy it is not to see, how easy to close a door when something is slightly off-kilter, stamping our own image on the disturbance, the image of the reality we know to be true.

But nonetheless there is something decidedly unnatural about the whole thing, her disproportionate doll-head, her evergreen garden, her stubborn immobility. Did she look out again? Was she brave enough? What did she see? Alison couldn't distinguish the woman's features, but somehow she could tell she was smiling. Between the shadows and the greenery she could glimpse the yellow shade of her small teeth.

Alison knew, at that moment precisely, that her neighbour would get her one day, exactly as Julian had predicted, and that she knew she would get her one day. They both know it; they had just been playing cat and mouse.

3.

Bad luck came with the house. A square building, four walls and a flat roof, part of a row of ugly nineteen-sixties terraced houses. The terrace sat at the end of a quaint street, opposite a much prettier row of Victorian two-bedroom cottages. The terraces were cheaply built, not enough insulation to cope with the heatwaves or the cold winter. It belonged to Julian's parents, and Alison and Julian had lived in the place for nearly two years, looked after it, spent a considerable amount of their own money on its upkeep.

The faults of the house were plenty. The north-facing back garden was a dark, shady patch of green, perpetually wet. There was a conservatory facing it. It wasn't badly put together, but it had certainly seen better days. When Alison and Julian first moved in, they discovered that one of the roof glass panels leaked. It cost them a small fortune to repair it, roughly Alison's monthly salary. The reality of the arrangement with Julian's parents had taken shape in front of her eyes at that moment. They owned the house, but they weren't landlords, did not want to behave like landlords, did not want to be bothered with problems. It was a rude awakening. Alison had not expected to have to come up with that kind of money for an urgent repair not covered by the already expensive house insurance. The whole thing left her stressed and worn out.

It had been the cost of the repair that had surprised her, and she would spend weeks agonising over one thing: the roof had six glass panels in total. What on earth would she do if they all started leaking? Would she have to spend half a year's salary fixing them? She lost sleep over this, took to obsessively checking the panels, heart leaping in her chest whenever it rained.

So that was it: they would live rent-free, but they would do everything that needed to be done, including paying whatever tax was due on the property, as well as being responsible for the home insurance Julian's parents had chosen, even if it did not cover the house's main problems. They were the problems of swift decrepitude, of the obsolescence of cheaply built places, of worn-out things; the typical problems of a house in need of endless rounds of maintenance, where all fixes were temporary, and something always needed to be done. Julian did not have a job yet, and Alison found herself paying for all the monthly bills and all repairs.

Alison would eventually grow to hate the house. It wasn't that she wasn't thankful to Julian's parents. The housing situation had reached almost catastrophe event levels: everyone she knew who owned property or rented within the town's perimeter was helped by some wealthier older relative. Some adjuncts had made headlines by living out of their cars. Garden sheds and garages and even old-fashioned bolthole-style disused bunkers in back gardens were rented out to young hourly-paid academics, the workforce who kept the town's illustrious institution going in exchange for no future retirement pay-outs, nor the job security necessary to put down roots and start a family. Meanwhile, academics from earlier generations, who were wealthier for the simple reason of having been born decades before, in the long-gone times of free education, a healthy job market, a free national health service at the point of need, were placidly sitting on half-empty properties all over town. The situation was untenable.

Alison did not feel comfortable for one simple reason: she had no legal way to prove that she lived in the house. A German national, the issue of proving residency to stay in the country turned out to be tricky. When Julian had mentioned the house, she had supposed there would be some kind of rental agreement in place; however, for some reason that Alison could not fathom, Julian's parents refused point-blank to draw up a contract. They did not want to be landlords, they repeated.

With rent-free living quarters, it made sense that Alison and Julian paid for everything. But there is nothing free in the world, of course, and her own payment was in the form of anxiety and fear, as Alison worried that without a contract she was not getting anywhere in terms of proving residency.

She consulted an immigration expert, gave him a copy of the letter Julian's parents had written to 'prove' she lived in the property. Her worst fears were realised when he explained such a document would not have any validity for her legal residency purposes. She agonised over the whole thing, found herself in her own personal limbo. The only role that was permitted to her was that of a passive enabler: she had to yield to others' decisions, and provide the money to put them into action. She might agree with something or not, or might wish that a particular item was changed or repaired, but she was not allowed to cast a vote. Every time she tried to suggest that something needed to be done, Julian would cut the problem off at the root by having a huge row with her. He was not very good at looking beyond his needs, and not happily drawn into conversations about things that did not interest him.

Alison could only look on, as things rapidly deteriorated around her: the black mould that infected most of the north-facing walls, the old stove that only worked when it wanted, with an extractor on top that did not work at all, the bad lighting in the kitchen which meant that they cooked in the dark and, most contentious of all, the lack of wardrobes and storage places.

Like a surprising number of English houses, the terrace was conspicuous for the absolute lack of closet space. As Alison understood it, before she and Julian were due to move in, his parents had suggested that a wardrobe of some sort needed to be built somewhere. However, for some reason this had never progressed from the planning stage, and the proposed closet never materialised. As a result, Alison kept her good clothes, the skirts and blouses and long dresses and cardigans she wore for work, in an array of dusty cardboard boxes that were spread around the little spare room and the landing. Then a strange dynamic brewed, one of those so typical of Julian and his family—impossible to anticipate, unavoidable, sticky once she was covered in it—where it became suddenly so easy to dismiss her opinions as irrationality: every time Alison asked when the wardrobes were going to be installed, she got a kind of exasperated look coming from Julian, who, most of his books up on shelves, had already forgotten everything about the need for some storage.

This saddened Alison. It reinforced her idea of how little Julian understood her life, the casual throwing around of words, 'alien,' 'migrant,' the endless questions and statements prefaced by the ubiquitous 'you are not from these parts.' It was painful to have confirmation of how little Julian understood, how little he knew, or cared to know. He was accusing her now of worrying too much about her clothing of all things, of being some sort of princess. This was ridiculous. Alison did not have many good clothes, or even expensive clothes, only the ones she used for work. Why was this so important, he repeated?

It was true, Alison tried to explain, that Julian turned up to meetings with editors—he was trying to become a translator—or with senior college tutors—he was trying to get some hourly-paid teaching going—in old t-shirts with holes in them, third-hand trousers straight out of charity shops, and shabby sports jackets inherited from his dad. But it was *he* who could sport this off-hand, shabby-chic manner of existing. Alison found it very difficult to explain to him in a way that he could understand, that he could relate to: with his blond hair, and his blue eyes, and his boyish smile, it did not matter what Julian was wearing, for he always belonged. Alison, a mixed-race foreigner, with 'not quite the right look' about her, as someone had once put it, was required to always appear immaculate. Very patiently, as if explaining something to a child, Alison had tried to clarify all this to Julian, how she had to prove she belonged three times more than him. How she needed to keep as neat and prim as possible merely to be taken seriously, to be considered professional rather than its opposite, to avoid the other not-so-pleasant monikers that quickly attached to her if she let her guard down.

She did not say other things, perhaps harder for him to understand, like how tiring it was to live like this, how exhausting it was to be constantly judged and prejudged. Alison was not sure at all that her husband of four years got any of it.

She had to do something. Eventually, Alison gave up and, trying to be practical, she spent some money on flat-pack wardrobes instead. She bought one for her clothes, one for Julian's, and another one to hang the coats and other heavy garments. When they arrived, she despaired. They were so badly designed that there were things that still did not fit in them, as now she realised there was also the linen to contend with, all the sheets and towels, that still had absolutely no place to go, and remained in the boxes. So Alison bought some plastic boxes as opposed to cardboard ones. They were piled up on the little landing. She reflected sadly on the situation: she was living in worse conditions than when she was a student. Julian at least was happy.

Sometimes events take on a life of their own. By then Alison was feeling overwhelmed beyond her worse nightmares. She could not have articulated the reason, but she found herself in tears every time she looked at her fat plastic boxes. Filled to the brim, they were so heavy that she could not handle them. Julian had to be asked to take them down from the pile, put them on the floor, put them back again in their pile, every time Alison needed to take something in and out of them. This, of course, exasperated him, put him on edge. He even accused her at some point of asking him to move boxes too often on purpose. If she did not ask him for help, he would also get offended, accusing her of hoping to drop one of the boxes on her foot, so she could have more reasons to complain. Hence, a further dynamic was established: whatever Alison did, or said, or didn't do, or didn't say, she would be sure of annoying him. And so it went on.

4.

Alison started imagining what she would do if Julian died; if he, for example, had a sudden heart attack. She would not be able to face telling her in-laws, who were sure to blame her and the whole sorry mess for it. Would she be better off putting him under the birch tree, with their unborn child? Or perhaps fit him in the bigger, sixty-four-litre plastic box?

Needless to say, a childish squabble over boxes wasn't everything. Sadly, things were still going to get much worse. Alison found herself in physical pain quite often, her immigration-related anxiety reaching astronomic proportions. Then Alison's unhappiness was the thing that started being questioned. The narrative went like this: Alison was, to all effects, a guest in the house, and should be nothing but grateful. Again, she felt that she could not explain properly, or that she would not be understood. Perhaps she was unhappy because Julian never allowed her to forget that she was a recipient of his charity. Without any unpleasantness, Julian knew how to place her under a sort of constant obligation to be grateful, and not to complain. There was no explicit uttering of this. All Julian had to do was to repeatedly mark his ownership of the place, subtly; but Alison understood. It was behind every assumption that he should not help with the upkeep, or even the cleaning, or that he was to be exempt from putting his shoes on the shoe rack under the stairs that she had bought, or even on a protective rug in the entry hall, but stubbornly out of it, leaving marks of mud on the carpeted floor that Alison was expected to clean. She was, in essence, assuming the awkward position of some kind of house-help in exchange for free rent. To try and avoid the unsavoury dynamic, Alison started insisting once more that she wanted to pay some rent, no matter how little. She didn't feel she could stand living like this, she insisted; unpleasant conversations ensued.

She started hating herself. How difficult would it be to live in a car, like those plucky adjuncts did? She had no money to go anywhere on her own, to fulfil her dream of renting a place, sign a piece of paper that stated she had an address, and to upload said piece of paper to the immigration portal. When, eventually, Julian's parents decided to put the house in his name, again he insisted that Alison should see it as some sort of lucky break that she had got thanks to him: now she would never be homeless in the ancient and overpriced town. But Alison could not reconcile her idea of herself with the narrative of leeching off her partner. That was not the way she wanted to think about herself. She had always had jobs and grants and scholarships, holding several part-time positions simultaneously at times. She had always felt proud of this part of her identity. Why did Julian insist on erasing it? Who was she, in fact, if he erased that? Someone she herself did not recognise, or wanted to know. Was Julian even aware that he was erasing that part of who she was, or had he never known her at all? He was not only forcing her to be exactly that person she despised, but also, cruelly, he was insisting that she should be grateful for being forced to become it.

She had shouted all of the above, but still there was no understanding from him. She felt utterly alone. Eventually, Julian called her an ungrateful bitch.

Still, she tried to explain once more that she was not being ungrateful, but simply that she had been forced into the rather uncomfortable position of losing control over her own life. In this, she felt, both Julian and his parents were equally to blame. As the argument worsened, Julian told Alison that he hoped she died in a ditch, and someone came and raped her dead body. Alison was so shocked by those words that she wrote them down in her notebook that evening, her whole body shaking. She did not want to forget that he had said them to her. 'Your smelly cadaver,' he had said, 'your stinking rotten cadaver.' This was the person she had almost had a baby with.

5.

She had, somehow, willed him to go. She could admit that much to herself. There was no coming back from the past few months.

Baptiste had noticed her loneliness, and he came up to her lap more often than ever. It was almost as if he was trying to comfort her. But he also spent the nights going up and down the stairs, his little paws going *clack clack clack* over the wooden floor, no doubt looking for Julian. But he was legally her cat, she thought, even if he had chosen Julian as his true owner. His companionship would not last long. Soon, he started getting thinner, and thinner, and thinner, until he weighed practically nothing. It was shocking to take him in her arms, a whole creature, no weight. Even a doll had more substance. Unable to go out into the world, Alison searched the web for extra special and expensive cat food to tempt him. He was gobbling it all up and yet still losing weight. The progress was fast, the vet shocked at his cadaveric expression when she saw him, alerting her that nothing was to be done as soon as she looked at him.

Still, she would see him after the end; many times she saw him. She at first thought that another cat had got into the house, when she first heard the *clack clack clack*. And then the animal jumped on her bed by the same corner Baptiste liked, and she felt the same non-weight on her body.

She was paralysed with something close to fear. Then, she fell asleep, and thought about it no longer.

Some days she would still hear him upstairs, hear the *clack clack clack* of his paws, see him leaving a room out of the corner of her eye. She put it all down to stress, loneliness.

She checked under the birch tree often, to make sure the earth looked the same. She decided she would plant the bulbs soon. This was a good, proactive idea. Then she went to have dinner, and, beans on toast on her lap, she tried to find something to watch. She was very proud of these little activities, which reinforced her capacity of acting 'normal'. She discovered that the streaming service did not work. The message on the screen was clear: the account had been discontinued. She remembered: this was one of the few things Julian had sorted, paid monthly from his own private account. It seemed that Julian had terminated their subscription. She would have to get it fixed. The whole idea was too much. She could read a book; but her reading pile had not gone down at all during the whole confinement. If anything, it looked bigger, more menacing, although she did not remember buying many books at all. It filled her with dread, feeling more guilty as the months passed, unable to read due to that guilt, the whole cycle perpetuating itself *ad nauseam*. Where did the books come from? She looked at them: they mostly had a library stamp. Had she taken them out, or Julian?

Alison went to bed earlier than she used to, and lay there, thinking. Waiting for the *clack clack clack* of her dead cat. Thinking about the birch tree at the edge of the back garden. And then she realised something: she hadn't had her period since Julian left. She truly hoped she wasn't pregnant, it would be too soon to do it all again: she had not yet managed to clean all the earth from under her nails. Perhaps her period had stopped due to stress. Perhaps her periods were ending. About time, she thought.

The problem of having a baby, Alison rationalised, was that, during the first few months of the baby's life, looking after a baby meant in fact succeeding in keeping the baby alive. And, Alison feared, she might not be up to protecting a newborn, or an infant, or a toddler, from peril. Or even worse, that Julian would wash his hands of it all, and she would not be able to cope on her own. There were other (irrational) fears, of losing the baby, somehow, to something that lurked in the shadows, among the crevices, in those liminal spaces we don't consider: landings, corners, spaces we use to go from room to room, or from her house to the vet, her only condoned outing in five months. A fear that there is a blank spot in all corners where the pavement becomes invisible for a second, and you cannot see the child anymore, only the brambles the council forgot to trim.

She lay there, thinking these thoughts. A friend had once explained how she saw a ghost one night while breastfeeding, but she was so tired it didn't matter. She could see the end of the stairs from her side of the king-size, where she sat at night to breastfeed, and they usually left the door of the bedroom ajar because they had a little kitty that wandered in and out of the room during the night, *clack clack clack*. One night she was sitting up breastfeeding, too sleepy to hold her head up, too tired to check her mobile phone. Then she saw her. A woman halfway up the flight of stairs, looking directly into the room, looking directly at her, a woman unknown to her, a dead woman. She says that was how her brain computed the information, almost mechanically. A woman who should not be there, conjured up in a little child's and mother's most sacred moment. There was something disturbingly meaningful about it. As soon as she was baby-free again she closed her eyes, not a second to lose from her precious sleep.

Alison looked to her slightly opened door, and found to her surprise that she could also see the end of the stairs into the little landing. She was waiting and waiting, until she heard the *clack clack clack*, the cadaveric expression, the dead cat jumping onto her lap, unable to leave entirely. And she knew, as her friend knew, mechanically, that he was protecting her, somehow.

She thought she saw her then, short, old and wrinkled, fiery white hair, dead eyes, pointy teeth. Alison was so scared at that moment that she levitated a few centimetres above the bed, pure energy finding a release through her pores. And then she fell asleep, and the next morning it was all long gone into the realm of nightmares and half-patched scraps of thoughts, ideas, securely interpreted as dreams. Still, she was beginning to understand something, to remember something. She just wasn't sure what, yet. Think Alison, think. It was very important to remember, to try to place this vague feeling. *Why did Julian leave me here?* No, that is not the question. *Why did Julian leave?*

6.

'Hello?' The telephone rang, would it be Julian? Alison had almost not answered. She could not remember the last time someone had rung the landline, as everyone communicated via apps that seemed to her progressively more and more difficult to understand.

'It's me, dear.' Alison's heart froze inside her chest. It was *her*. Why was she calling? 'I was wondering if Julian could do something for me.'

'Julian is not in, not right now.' She was very careful not to give away the truth, that she was completely, indefinitely, alone. 'Can I help?'

It was nothing, nothing at all. And she was so sorry to bother Alison. But the thing was, there was a continuous scurrying sound in the space between the two houses, a narrow gap between her wooden garden fence and the brick wall that had been added to Julian's house to build the conservatory. A trapped rat, or a hedgehog.

Alison's stomach contracted. She had been so worried about rats, almost obsessively. Since the confinements started, and due to the inactivity in the streets, the closed restaurants and shops, rats had become bolder. Without their usual supply of rubbish they had got closer to houses than ever, sometimes even getting into them in their search for food. Alison was forced to open the windows regularly in her ongoing fight with the black mould, but she was terrified when she did so. What if a rat, or rats, were going to get in? She usually sat at the end of the sofa to read or to knit or to watch television, as close to the wall as possible, the warmest spot in the room. And yes, now that she thought about it, she had heard the noise many times in the previous few days. Could there really be rats trapped there? Until now, she had imagined them climbing the outer wall. But then, this could only be her imagination; for she could also imagine *her* climbing the outside wall, feasting on the rats, listening inside Alison's house.

Her neighbour explained once again, in case Alison's English was not up to scratch. That she thought the noise came from a small animal, trapped between the brick wall of their conservatory and her garden fence. But she was too old and could not navigate the narrow space, did Alison understand?

'Do you understand, dear? I need you to go and look, and do whatever needs to be done. Or you can always send Julian when he is back home.'

She had obviously done it on purpose. The whole conversation sounded like a way to get Alison to acknowledge that she could not do it because she was on her own. Or maybe she had brought the rats somehow to torment Alison.

She said that she would go. She was too scared to come clean about Julian's desertion. Although something told her that her neighbour knew.

If Julian were here, he would laugh at her so hard, at her strange fears of the little, harmless lady. But then again, he had also put the idea in her head, that the old lady would come to get her. So she put her rubber boots on, took a torch from the kitchen drawer, and set out. And out she went, to look around the conservatory. Thick bushes, undergrowth. The fear of small baby rats, of rats' nests, biting at her feet. Impossible to advance without damaging her cardigan, without catching it on the branches. And then the narrow stretch, impossible to see the dark ending, manoeuvring herself inside without thinking.

She became trapped, momentarily. And the world stopped for a moment. Unable to move, her brain started racing, how to suss her body out, little by little. She could do it, if she wasn't so anxious. She only needed to calm down, which in turn increased her anxiety.

What is the scurrying, right there? Like the sound of a knife scratching a china plate.

She sees it then, the diamond of light, kaleidoscopic shapes that dance among themselves, opening the point in space to her, and she sees it, all that there is to see, and she understands.

Before passing, Julian's hand had stopped in a sort of rictus, a scratching position. What was he doing, hiding in here? Was he hiding from the witch, or from Alison? And Alison, she will make it out, won't she?

There is a thought for her baby. What exactly, about it? What exactly about her and her baby?

She cannot remember.

What Would Kate Bush Do?

I.

Woman, mid-thirties.
Two-thousand-five.
November.
Afternoon.
Tired by TV and biscuits
she goes to her boyfriend's bathtub,
empty, and stays there.
The boyfriend feeds her
(kebabs, burgers, curry).
Dear, are you coming out?
Perhaps tomorrow, my love.
A day later. Two years later.
When the firemen remove her
her skin sticks to the porcelain.
What do I need, you ask?

A little understanding, deeper.
And love, please.

II.

Woman, seventy?
Could be seventy.
She was eight,
she was nine.
Not sure at all.
Cleaned the doctor's house,
one shilling a week.

Five shillings gone—
stolen, lost, vanished?
Who cares.
They say ...
they say she's responsible.

This show costs five shillings:
Come and See!
Ladies and Gentleman!
Come and See!
Come to the Lunatic Asylum!
See the Incurable
Morbid
Criminal!
No one remembers,
really remembers,
why she is here.

No one remembers
and nobody cares.
Five shillings:
a cheap ticket for a show
that lasts a whole life.
You can't stop it,
can't come off the wheel.
Isn't it fun?
It's fun, isn't it?
(Reform school;
Mental Hospital;
Asylum for the forgotten.)
She's twenty, she's thirty,
she's fifty, sixty ...
Could be seventy.
Who cares? No one remembers.
Her family finds her:
she doesn't know them,
doesn't know herself,
doesn't know the country she lives in.
What a country is.
Could it be possible, dear,
to swap places at some point?

III.

Woman, forty-two,
Musician.
Dead.
Five years later

she's the world's leading pianist.
(Hang on! Wasn't she dead?)
Each LP unique,
unrepeatable:
a genius told by another genius.
She is ...
ill.
She is ...
a recluse,
bent in her studio,
recording the marvels
of her grandiose loneliness.
So pretentious ...
The story is different.
The story is Indjic, Nojima, Ashkenazy,
and her husband,
and a computer.
Digital edition,
unique collage.
And me, wishing a sound could kill ...

IV.

The seven-year-old is interrogated alone.
Her mother diminishes in jail
(she still appears to her daughter as a black cat).
She confesses, the child, to have been a witch
    since she was six:
she is not sure if she is seven or eight now.
    But she is sure of being a witch.

She tries to be clever in front of the
illustrious men:
if they say
things are happening, then surely they are.
Who is she, a little girl, to go against them?
Her replies are bright, articulate.
She is enjoying her rare moment of glory.
When a judge
a pastor, a reverend, a magistrate
(a man)
decides you have done something,
a whole new memory develops.
Women who swallow, and process, and spew up,
history, folklore, myths,
malicious town gossip,
recycle it all to feed the men,
the vast mouths of power,
hope that if they give them what they want
they will be saved.
Can they be, saved?
Can we please, please, wake the damn witch now?

v.

Woman, seventeen.
Have you ever run
to save your life?
She had to,
crossing the highway
into a dirty forest.

All Europe is the same labyrinth
of dark corridors,
red bulbs,
locked rooms,
secret rooms,
rooms of pain and desire ...
empty fields, vans,
and nameless men.
Boundaries, frontiers:
(she thinks she crosses them,
doesn't know for sure.
Who cares?).
The room is always the same room.
The men are always the same men.
Five of them, six, seven, eight ...
A doll, a slave.
The whole of Europe: a vast dirty room
locked inside a forest.
The sink, the sheets, all equal;
the same fields, the same van,
and men, exactly the same.
Will the pendulum ever swing?

Out of the Window, Into the Dark

Be bold, be bold, but not too bold,
Lest that your heart's blood should run cold.
—Traditional English Tale

When I was growing up there was a series of comics I was obsessed with. It was called *Out of the Window, Into the Dark*. I wasn't the only one, all kids my age were under its spell during one of those unmemorable summers when we had nothing much to occupy ourselves with. No one knew who wrote it and drew it: it was enigmatically signed by 'The Knocker-Up', and published by some obscure press we had never heard of, The Amber Press, which didn't even sound like a comic book press at all if you ask me. The unusual goings-on did not end there. Unlike other comic book series, no one knew when the next instalment was going to be published. Neither me nor my friends remembered how or when we had come to hear about it, or how it had fallen on our laps. To top it all, some inner instinct told us that our parents would not approve of it, so we kept it a secret.

We weren't bad kids, at least not when it all started. But I would say that all kids, in general, learn to keep their parents in the dark from some of the stuff they do, things they read and see. What is the reason for that? Probably because all kids have a misplaced sense of what they can control, of which situations, dangerous or otherwise, they can manage successfully. The problems start when it becomes clear you have no control at all, and find yourself in danger, perhaps even in 'mortal peril', that horrific phrase made quaint by readings of *The Happy Hollisters* from the local library. Needless to say, by the moment you come to the realisation that you are in 'mortal peril', it would be probably too late.

We all know the kind of stories, the kind of situations that I am taking about. Our town hadn't invented putting the faces of lost children on milk cartons. Me, Pete, and the others. Fast friends as the pariahs, the uncool kids who did not do sports or excel at anything. Those who sit silently in the middle to last row in the classroom. I guess we came pretty close to disaster on a few memorable occasions, and of course there were some lucky escapes. Or, perhaps, the worst wasn't meant to happen to us after all. Not because we didn't try: we liked racing along the trainlines with our bikes, we played dangerously close to the Electric

Towers despite being told now and again not to go near them, and a kid we all knew had drowned in the canal two summers before on a dare during a particularly hot weekend. Needless to say, we had also been swimming in the same spot a couple of hours before, splashing and fighting and jumping in the water without a care in the world. However, the time we came closer to actual peril was when the incident with Odd Paul happened. We didn't tell anyone, and no one ever knew how close to danger we had been. No one knew how we were connected to the tragic events of that day either, the day when Odd Paul spontaneously combusted in the back garden of his 1930s semi.

I guess by then we were a bunch of nervous, edgy kids. As we never knew when the next instalment of *Out of the Window, Into the Dark* was going to be published, the constant guessing made us even more eager, at times the anticipation could have been misconstrued as panic. To add to the complication, such sophisticated piece of art did not reach our sleepy town. We were lucky: Pete's older brother happened to have a weekend job selling frozen yogurt in a shopping centre two suburbs away. There was no good bus connection to get there, so each Saturday morning his mother drove him over while he tried to get his driver's licence. The shopping centre had quite a large comic book shop. Whenever he got us a new instalment, he insisted that we paid him a little extra over the retail price for the favour, which placed us in a precarious position. We were always coming up with different schemes to raise the extra cash, from collecting and selling empty glass bottles, to taking the rubbish bins out for old ladies on collection day, or finding their missing cats. And all this extra money went into a box that we all kept in turns, to make it as fair as possible. We didn't want to think what would happen if Pete's brother, who was pretty much an idiot, realised one day the power he was sitting upon, and how he could in fact turn his little money-making scheme into extortion in the blink of an eye. By then we were hooked. *Out of the Window, Into the Dark* had us under its spell.

Eventually, one of our parents caught us reading the comic. To say that they were shocked was the understatement of the year. There were phone calls between our parents, and it was decided that we were not going to read it anymore. It was their opinion that *Out of the Window, Into the Dark* wasn't appropriate reading materials for a bunch of kids. For a kiddies comic book, they thought, it was surprisingly dark, a dark collection of rather dark stories, probably not for kids at all to start with. The stories followed a similar pattern. The hero looked into houses at children's windows, preferably at night, when the kid's parents were asleep. He floated in mid-air, and knocked on the glass, helped the children climb out of the window, and then he took them with him, invariably to see something or other that the kid was not meant to see.

What do I mean by that? Well, as well as we had ways of keeping our parents in the dark from certain of the things we did, there were things that our parents tried very hard to keep us from. All towns have plenty of those, incidents that parents hide from the impressionable little ones, things that we were not meant to know, not meant to hear, definitely not meant to see.

In our town, this translated as a series of chapters in a semi-hidden, and rarely acknowledged story, each darker than the next. Some of them come to mind, even now: the grim tale of some kids, not much older than us, who had been killed ten years previously while doing their shift in the petrol station at the entrance of town. Or that school open secret that someone's dad, a kid from the class below us, met the piano teacher in the apartment-hotel on the outskirts of the A-14. Or perhaps even that my mother did not lose our puppy, but abandoned it ... Although this one would have been very difficult to call 'hidden', as my mother chose to do this while I was in the car. She calmly stopped in a bypass, opened the back door, took him out of my arms, put it on the floor outside the car, and drove off, ignoring my innocent remarks that the little puppy—writing his name is too painful even now—could possibly not keep up with us, and please to stop and let him in the car again. The last images of the animal, fighting to keep up, slowly getting swallowed up and forever lost between the grey cars, still burns in my retina. Or else the lies, everywhere abundant, which children are fed until an embarrassingly late age. For example, that well-spread one that decrees that when parents divorce, apparently you are not only not to blame, but somehow they will both continue loving you unconditionally. As if love wasn't a commodity with a sell-by date, or as if adults, parents in particular, did not get bored of their offspring, tired of looking back into half-baked, misguided previous versions of their lives, those ones that they were so eager to leave behind. At least this one particular lie is ever easier to spot: soon the absent father contents himself with Family Number Two, and you become not much more than the leftovers.

There is more, so much more. Two kids run over; their mother, now an old lady, braving the outside despite the gravel and rotten vegetables thrown at her by children not much older than the ones she lost, unsteadily walking towards the crossing where she leaves yet another supermarket bouquet to wilt next to some faded pictures where you can see two faces if you try very hard, and a couple of soggy teddies.

The girl abducted on her birthday, found exactly a year later, but not a year older.

The mother who set fire to her bungalow because her husband was going to kill her and her daughter.

The boy who made a perfect noose in the Boy Scouts meeting, and, afterwards, use it put at end to it all, precisely in order to escape from the Scout leader, kumbaya and all.

All those incidents that our parents somehow thought we were oblivious to, knew nothing about, when in fact they were our breast-milk. We grew up with those very tales. They made us into the men and women we are now, either entirely desensitised to pain, or hugely aware of it. None of those two options being ideal.

Now that I am older, I am aware that all towns are branded by fire with stories very similar to those. That dark legacy is their true history. But, when we were little, we naively thought our local woes were unique. We truly believed no other school boasted the ghost of a bullied kid living in a haunted bathroom cubicle. Or that no other place in the world possessed an abandoned fairground as scary as ours, at a time when the failing economy, hitting us right in the face after the buoyancy of the previous decades, when arcades, play parks, camps, had sprouted like mushrooms everywhere, only to become during our own childhoods shadows of themselves, liminal, abandoned places. Or that no other neighbourhood but ours had its own empty house, a back garden grown out of proportion, grass higher than we. Empty rooms. Half-opened closets into nothingness. Never-ending darkness. We used those scenarios to dare us into the unknown. We liked the chills of this sought-for terror. We enjoyed Halloween and all its *papier mâché* scares, not understanding that, all along, the devil was living two streets up ahead, and the mouth of hell had opened up many times in the past few years directly from his garden shed. This devil was no other than Odd Paul.

By then, Odd Paul had progressed in our heads from harmless local weirdo, to improbable dark hero, all this before he would turn to our worst nightmare, exactly in that order. We had given him an imagined origin story, connected of course with our number one obsession, *Out of the Window, Into the Dark*. It happened like this: not knowing that these stories are as common as pain, that every town in the world had a few of them, and then a few more sprinkled on top, someone suggested one day that the tales in *Out of the Window* were so close to our local darkest experiences, that the writer *had* to live in our very town. This was an exciting theory. It was also scary; but scary like Halloween was scary, nice thrills, consumed from afar. We bowed to find him. We prepped like kids our age did in movies, with backpacks filled with battery torches, walkie-talkies, a secret code composed of different words, our trusted bikes, in case making an escape became necessary. We hunted through the shopping centre, the local library, the newsagents. We had fun for a while, although we had no idea what we were doing, and soon would be completely out of our depth. This is how we became aware of Odd Paul. We started keeping an eye in people around us, even following some on occasion. We were spying on our neighbours, and this was how we found him, on the local library, one Saturday morning.

Odd Paul had no job that we knew of. He lived in a semi that had belonged to his mother. His house was the last in a row of terraces, generally well-kept, flower beds and trimmed hedges and no rubbish or old furniture on sight. Rubbish bins tastefully kept at the back of the houses, pavement cleanish, tea and family dinner and *Countdown* punctually behind half-drawn curtains, or none at all. In this context, his house was the odd one out. It wasn't necessarily kept in disrepair, mind you; but, if you looked carefully, you could see that the short front garden was a little more overgrown than necessary, that the windows were not as spotless, that the odd tile was falling down. Still, nothing noticeable, or at least nothing that would be noticeable in another couple of years at least. Neglect had not entirely arrived, but was getting there insidiously. Later on, during the police investigation, it would come out that Paul was unemployed, and studied at night in the local community college; odd topics, such as Global History and Polish, while drawing some kind of benefit. We knew nothing of this. To us, he was simply a solitary guy, with the time and the space to embark in a project such as this one. We followed him over a couple of days. He liked spending time in the local library every week, sitting there reading magazines and newspapers, and, like the amateur detectives we fancied ourselves to be, we even managed to find out which books he was fond of checking out: boring, History. However, one of the mornings spent in the library shadowing him, a dull, grey Saturday with an overcast Summer sky, was also when we decided that he could not be our guy: Pete had managed to get a drawing he had left behind, little more than a doodle, but which made us conclude that he could not be the artist behind our loved comic book. He had absolutely no talent. We quickly forgot about him.

At least, my friends forgot about him. Something about Odd Paul still seemed to linger in my brain for weeks afterwards. During the night, he was present in my nightmares. During the day, I carefully avoided thinking about him. Doing so gave me an uncomfortable feeling at the pit of my stomach, as if I was still expected to find something, as if we had not finished our business with him. Something, in short, unexpected. Was Odd Paul becoming my own obsession? Things came to a head when I was sick for a week, the last week of the summer. It was a week of unseasonable weather, quite dark and foreboding and still August. Late-summer storms had conspired to darken the general mood. It was, in short, a strange-weather week at a time when we knew nothing of strange weather. And, for that, it felt unique, as if the world was aligning itself with my ill-timed flu. Who had flu at the end of the summer, anyway?

Well, not me. That is for sure. Our elderly doctor had mistakenly prescribed antibiotics, the last thing he should have done. I could not breathe, my glands swelled up to gargantuan proportions. I had hallucinations, I was raving with fever. Unknown to everyone, what I had was glandular fever, and the antibiotics almost killed me.

Something happened. Was it a hallucination, or else my brain conveying some kind of information? I would never know. I was lying in bed, in my room. I hated my room. My mum had insisted on painting it pink when I was little, even if I had never liked pink. Still, a girl meant a 'pink room'; that was the extent of her imagination. I felt as if I was sleeping inside a gigantic half-chewed piece of bubblegum, or even worse, somebody's guts. I felt as if I had been eaten up. The psychedelic pink room did not help my dreams, even less those that I had due to the ill-timed antibiotics. I remember two things from those hallucinatory hours: a peddler that came round my neighbourhood sometimes, perched on the top of my wardrobe (obviously, he wasn't there), beating a drum, drum, drum; the little purple dots of my duvet cover holding hands and spinning in circles to its tune in some strange May dance. And the traveller, of course, directly out of *Out of the Window, Into the Dark*, knocking at my very window.

The most obsessive amongst us, that is, Pete and myself, had of course found out what 'knocker-up', the alleged author of the series, meant. It turned out to be an old profession, heading from Victorian times. Apparently, 'knockers-up' went from house to house, tapping on windows with their long sticks, to make sure people woke up in time to get to their jobs. It made sense: the Victorian poor, in their slums, did not have the luxury of alarm clocks, of course.

This now made perfect sense to me in my delirium. I knew somehow that I had unfinished business with Odd Paul, and so, I shouted at the man behind the glass: 'Is it time? Is it time to go now?' To which he answered with a nod.

I should say that he wasn't Odd Paul, that much was clear. Still, what we had been trying to determine was whether Odd Paul was the author, not the 'actual' traveller ... But things were getting mixed up inside my head.

The traveller opened the window and invited me out, and suddenly I was floating in his direction, in that way you do in dreams.

The rest is odd to explain, ever odder than Odd Paul himself. I tried to do so in the following days many times to my friends; not to my mother, or to the police. But to them I owed this. Still, it was a strange thing, slightly surreal. A dream, of course. But then, I could not explain how I knew what I later knew. Could it be because I knew it, or suspected, somehow from before, and the fever drew up the knowledge? Could it be because I had imagined it somehow, feared it?

So, the thing is, the traveller took me to see something I should not see, of course; and it turned out to take me directly to Odd Paul's house; and we floated around it, towards the back garden; and once there we floated directly on the shed; and then we went 'through' the shed roof, as in a dream – for it was a dream – or rather as if we were ghosts.

And then I saw him, lying there, the last lost boy from the last milk cartoon.

There was only one thing we could do: we would rescue the boy.

The next week I felt better. I met my friends in the play park, a patch of yellow grass with gaping holes and metal bar contraptions with brightly coloured paint peeling. We kicked a can around, stood on the back wheel of our bikes, shared a cigarette someone had gotten from her mum's purse.

The first thing I had to do was convincing them that we should go take a look. To my friends, my dream had been exactly that, a dream. To me, it had been a vivid scene, and somehow I felt I had flew there and seen the boy.

Sneaking into Odd Paul's garden wasn't difficult. Later on, I would have wished that it had been. Breaking into the shed took us an awful long time, more than movies and TV shows had suggested. But break into we did, as silently as we could manage. So silently the main sound were our gasps of horror at what we found there.

The boy was there alright, a short, scraggy thing, of a dark rubbery unwashed colour, lying on a heap of blankets in a corner. The smell was indescribable, and we all gagged. It brought something to mind, but only much later on I recognised its soft edges, the taste at the tip of my tongue: the zebras in the zoo. The zebras I had seen when my father took me there with his new family. It was the twins' fourth birthday, and they had chosen themselves what they wanted to do. An outing I would never forget.

The story does not end there. Of course, we weren't as silent or as clever as we had hoped, and of course Odd Paul found us in the act. The rest is history: his tall, thin figure blocking the door, the ominous rope he kept stretching and playing with in his hands. The realisation that it was the end. The bargain we made with the devil then and there.

Somehow, we convinced him that he could let us go, that is, except the little boy. I am not proud of this, and his contorted face, the pain after the hope, was so unbearable that I deliberately looked away from him, into the monster I was speaking to. I am not sure who made me the leader, and perhaps I was not the leader after all. But something had happened to me during my illness. Somehow, I did not care anymore, as if a part of my brain, the one that dealt with primal terror, the one instinct destined to save us in the jungle, had somehow shrunk. I had put my friends in that position, I would take them out of it. Also, I thought to myself, I was only gaining time. How and when I would rescue the boy after that remained to be seen. But, somehow, if I managed to gain some time, I could think about it later. I would have wished that I could convey, by some form of telepathy, all of this to the boy. Of course, telepathy does not exist.

I struck a bargain, then and there. I have never been so inspired before in my life, and I know I peaked at that moment, and that I would never be cleverer or better or more decisive than I was that night. In short, that was the single moment of excellence in my life and, from then on, quite rightly, I entered a descending curve. All I said to him was: we will go now. But we will bring someone to take our place. And, since we had done that for you, we will become your accomplices, and we will not be able to tell anything about what we have seen. You can be sure of that.

And then he said, okay. But you will bring me someone every year.

And then we said, what?

Well, that was my friends. I said, okay, we will. They looked at me in terror. I left with Pete, the others staying behind for accountability. Their faces. We were happy to leave my friends there as security, for we knew that I would uphold our side of the bargain. But, again, I would have liked it if telepathy had existed.

Pete and me talked about it, thought of a plan. It was simple, it was beautiful. We were happy to leave the small child there, for we said to ourselves it was only for the time being, we would come back for him. We were happy to agree to a yearly offering, for we reasoned that we would have a whole year to find a way to trick the devil.

Or perhaps it just was that we were bad people.

Pete and me went out, and we found a telephone box, and phoned Pete's house, and he made his brother come to find us. The same brother that was now charging us the moon and the stars for every comic. That would teach him, right? Killing two birds with one stone, right? We thought we were so clever ...

But I got ahead of myself. We weren't going to give Pete's brother, or exchange him. We weren't in the mood to subject ourselves to yet another fucked up power struggle with yet another authority figure. I rallied my troops. Pete and his brother. I probably still had some lingering fever on me. Or that deformation in my brain due to my illness. Pete's brother brought the things we had asked, three balloons filled with fire accelerator from the family barbecue, and three lighters. The rest was meant to be simple. And beautiful. Or so I kept repeating.

We would only have one chance to get it right.

We got back, Pete's brother pretending all the time that he didn't know what was going on. Odd Paul was waiting for us. We were lucky: he was waiting for us in the middle of the garden. I had feared he might have been still inside the shed. This would have made it all much more complicated and potentially dangerous.

I guess we went a bit overboard with him. I suppose that is an accurate description of what happened. Three small balloons filled with accelerant turned out to be too much. We just wanted to scare him, inflict some burns, make sure he would bolt town. We never, in a million years, wanted to kill him. That was not what we planned to do. You have to believe me.

But something took hold of me when I saw him, a sudden rage. For the kids in the petrol station ten years earlier, the brother and sister in the hit and run, my father, the twins. Odd Paul had started talking, I don't even know what he was on about, when I went ahead and threw my balloon at him. This was unscripted: we had previously decided on a different course of action. But I panicked. Let the rage flow freely on me. Odd Paul did not react at first. Being bombarded with bright red balloons that say 'happy retirement' filled with liquid may not have been what he was expecting to happen. It must have taken him a few seconds to realise that they did not have water after all. He was tasting the accelerator right on his face: Pete's brother had smashed his balloon full on it. Odd Paul now advanced towards us, menacingly, and Pete's brother, nonchalantly, flicked his lighter at him. It was a light flick, lasting less than one second, I wasn't even sure there had been any contact between the flame and the drenched man. As it happened, it turned out to be more than enough contact. Odd Paul lit up.

Again, this was completely unscripted: what we had agreed was that we would all throw our lighters in Odd Paul's direction. At the end, no lighter was thrown at him, which meant that there were less things left behind to link him to us.

Our friends were waiting in the shed, and we took them out. Pete's older brother had finally passed his driver's test, and he took the child into hospital, leaving him by the door.

After all these years it is still strange to talk about these events. I know we did something awful, which changed us all forever. Sometimes I wonder if there is a connection between that night, and the fact that I am sleeping here of all places. I also know that it was us or him, kill or die, survival of the strongest. Or something like that.

That is all that is to tell. Not quite. We soon heard from the news how it all ended. The boy, in the hospital. There was quite a commotion when they found out who he was. He claimed he had walked all the way to the hospital from Odd Paul's house. He repeated over and over one thing, that the man had 'started burning' of his own accord. How? They asked. Just burning, by himself.

Before the local police could get control of the narrative, the local press went ahead with this story. Soon, the national newspapers were talking about the 'spontaneous combustion' incident in our town. Experts flooded our television screens, analysing if the impossible could have become, by some miracle, possible. TV anchors prioritised this narrative of events: boy miraculously saved, villain touched by the angry finger of God. We were glued to the reports and round tables speaking of it all, to the same footage of Odd Paul's house which was played on a loop, all the time fearing that the undersign right below it, in bright reds and shiny whites, with a thick black font shouting *'Breaking!'*, would give us away at any minute. Each time a siren was heard in our streets, or even further away, we feared they were coming for us.

The boy said nothing about us. We are sure that the police experts found the accelerant, or what remained of it, in the ash heap that had been Odd Paul. Or, perhaps, the police department had proved to be as unimaginative as our parents, who suspected nothing, imagined nothing. Eventually, as summer ended, and, as the autumn leaves filled the suburban streets, a serial cat killer took hold of our town's imagination. And so ended the short reign of the 'Spontaneous Combustion Mystery'.

I have never told this to anyone. That year, for whatever reason, we all dispersed amongst new friends and pursuits. I took up soccer: I had a lot of energy that needed an outlet. I slept badly most nights, except the ones when I tired myself to death on the pitch, so I took strongly to the sport, of course. Pete's old brother went to Uni in a coastal town out West. I saw him once during the Christmas break, from afar, in a Sainsbury's parking lot. We nodded at each other, and that was it.

I could tell that the girl he was with was asking who the hell I was.

No, that is not it. Things are never that simple, are there? I felt it again, eventually. My own fear, changing the edges of things, turning them blurry. As if a soft membrane between objects and their meanings was being pulled out. I could not find any other explanation why I knew the boy was where he was. And then it happened again. That fever, the wrongly-prescribed antibiotics. They did shift something inside my adolescent brain, something definitive. Shifting or unlocking, I haven't yet made up my mind. The thing is, every time I have a fever, I have one of those ominous, horrific visions. They come to me like horrid local tales, and I see children, and teenagers, and women, and cats, and dogs, and all sorts of things. Everything, in detail. I tried to escape it, going to the big city; but, once there, the cacophony was simply impossible. So I left the city, and went to a scarcely populated rural area. Living there was even worse: now I could see the most horrid secrets of people I saw and greeted daily. There weren't many of us around. So, after all, I ended up coming back here instead. I got a job in the local library, and stayed out of trouble. More importantly, I tried very hard to stay healthy, and I can happily say I hardly ever suffer from high fever. One day I saw that Odd Paul's house was going to be sold in public auction, and I could not resist it. I guess it is normal to want to come back permanently to the place of your moment of highest glory.

I didn't read the comic again, I went completely off it. The strangest thing happened, many years later. I have asked several people my age, and no one seems to know anything about the series, or had heard anything about a comic book called *Out of the Window, Into the Dark*, or has ever seen it anywhere. I have tried to look for it in specialised second-hand bookshops, online, I have attended collectors' events, I have even searched librarian databases. Nothing. I also looked for The Amber Press for a while, but never found it. It is as if they had vanished in mid-air, or else they never existed.

I think often about our actions. How could we do such a thing, so easily? That day, we left our houses as children, looking for a monster of sorts, only to end up becoming the monsters ourselves. As if all we had found was a shiny mirror to discover who we really were.

There are some mornings when I wake up and the sky looks ominous, as if what we did is painted on it. There are some days when I see dragons, floating in front of my eyes. There are nights when it is impossible to sleep. Those nights sting more than I can say. The smell, I could never forget it. I have been a vegetarian for the last forty years.

Blake's Wife

All the poison I convert it and I turn it to love
—The Last Dinner Party

Europe, a prophecy, Copy 'M', c. 1832, Fitzwilliam Museum, Cambridge University

I stood in front of copy 'M' of *Europe, a Prophecy*. And after waiting so long to see it, I wasn't giving it my full attention. My mind kept wandering, musing on a bizarre label, present on a great number of exhibits that morning: *'Allocated by H.M. Treasury through the Ministry of the Arts, after acceptance in lieu of capital taxes, 1985'*. Copy 'M' did not in fact bear this legend, but a great number of the other precious objects in this exhibition, a major Blake exhibition, did. And so my mind wandered on the improbable journey of some of these treasures, on the eternal question of who has access to them, and of how access comes to the rest of us—sometimes by mere chance, by someone needing to perform an action so unpoetic as paying taxes to the English nation. The improbability of it all. I was reminded of that time when I was trying to get access to the National Library in Madrid, the lady in reception explaining that it was not possible 'just to use the library'. This was alarming. Wasn't the library meant to be Spain's national collection, built and kept and curated for us, its citizens? Although I have a Spanish passport, I am a dual citizen, a 'half-citizen'. Maybe they could allow me access to *half* the collection...? The absurdity of it all.

They gave me a reader's card eventually, but I had to come back with a letter from my supervisor explaining that I needed to consult the collection for my studies. The episode left a bad taste in my mouth.

Behind me, my partner pushed back his glasses and read the exhibition catalogue, pretending he didn't know me. I am a sucker for blue-eyed intellectual men with glasses. I blame a long-lost love. I had never liked men with glasses until I slept with this boy, and since then I have not been able to stop myself finding this particular type sexy. My new partner... I was not sure he was my partner, exactly. He already had a girlfriend, a fiancée in fact. We had contrived to enter the exhibition at the same time, but we had to be careful not to be seen chatting too much, not to be seen too intimate with each other. There was also the issue that he was my direct supervisor in my part-time evening job at the University Library. He had access to some of its most precious books. Now, that was sexy! I fantasised about kissing him among the stacks of expensive medieval manuscripts, of making love to him hidden away behind the shelves. That would never happen, of course: too risky. When he brushed me lightly when passing behind me, I felt a shiver of happiness and lust mixed together.

'MY SHADOW OF DELIGHT'

In Cambridge, I had hoped to see copy 'M' of *Europe, a Prophecy*, after reading something that I found astonishing: that the copies labelled 'I', 'L' and 'M', held at the Huntington Library, the Auckland Public Library, and the Fitzwilliam, the University Museum of the town where I lived, were all posthumous copies, printed after Blake's death in 1827. Copy 'M', in fact, had been printed five years afterwards, in 1832. *Ergo*, Blake himself had not been involved in its production. I had been fishing around for a dissertation topic. In truth, I had been fishing around for a *new* topic. So far, I had tried to write summaries and proposals of the following ideas: a comparative study of the aesthetics of Poe and Borges; a treatise on visual narrative in medieval manuscripts; and something vague about fairy-tales. Unsurprisingly, my partner didn't take any of this seriously—not the topics in themselves, but the fact that I kept changing and changing, seemingly unable to commit to anything. If I didn't decide soon, a very final, unmissable deadline would in fact be missed. I would not complete my graduate course, which would lead to, probably, being stuck in low-paid library work for ever and ever and ever, unable to progress to the kind of managerial job he had. He had a fancy PhD, called a DPhil, from the other place.

In bed, I tried to explain my last obsession, and, to be fair, he tried to listen. It might be possible to fall in love with Blake without loving the fact that he produced his books, that he manufactured, from start to finish, these astonishing art works. It might be possible to understand Blake fully as a poet without appreciating him as a printer and an artist. But, to me the sublimity of the pieces made it difficult. I was in awe of these delicate objects that expressed so much, so powerfully, in such small format, the thing itself a work of genius as much as the poems inside it. The magnitude of his achievement in creating these objects made it impossible. And then ... there was the matter of his wife Catherine, her role in the press. Why not write about her? He snorted. What about her? Maybe I needed to do more research before mentioning Catherine to him ...

This topic suited me exceedingly. I have always been interested in books as objects, in their provenance, in how they are put together, in who owns them, in collections, in the material aspects of it all. I print and bind books, in an amateur, embarrassing way: I inherited a printing press from an elderly aunt. I am still not sure why she thought I should have it. A nice man from Yorkshire called Steve transported it, piece by piece, and built it, piece by piece, inside the shed of the semi I share with other graduate students. It took him half a day to put it together, but at the end, there it was, a rather pretty, I would even say feminine, early Victorian Columbian Press, with an eagle on top. It was love at first sight. I am a graduate student, and my survival has not always depended on grants: I've worked in every aspect of the book trade, in an astonishingly short number of years. I've written a couple of short story books, and I've translated things between Spanish and English; but I've also worked as an editor, and even had a short stint as a publisher, covering a maternity leave, although I found that particular line of work far too stressful. I've learnt to bind and repair books, and I've worked in libraries for years and years, all through my undergraduate years and now, as a graduate student. I've even undergone training as a rare book trader, and I've sold books on occasion. And, of course, I collect them. I am drawn to handmade things, signed editions, unique bindings, beautiful experiments. I collect kitchen-table zines that I buy on Etsy; *cartonera* publications that come all the way from Mexico, from Bolivia, from Peru; I am always scanning book fairs for unusually bound volumes; and I've even managed to build a small but precious collection of signed modern firsts. I've been known to spend necessary grant money on a signed Rachel Ingram, or else a poetry prize on a first edition, signed copy of *The Bloody Chamber*. But that was when I was younger and had fewer worries: I wouldn't do it now.

My entry point into Catherine Blake as a possible dissertation topic was the idea that understanding words and images must surely go together in Blake's case. A copy of *Songs of Innocence and Experience* was going up for auction in New York. Curious, I checked the estimate: between one and one-and-a-half million dollars (it sold for just under a million). So, obviously, I argued, not *any* book of poems, but rather this sublime, delicate, impossibly exquisitely produced dainty tome. And it was labelled by the auction house, rather gracefully in my opinion, *William [and Catherine] Blake, c. 1789*. The use of those square brackets pleased me exceedingly, they seemed to prove my point. Blake wasn't dead in 1789; but somehow, somewhere, a curator had understood that the production of this fine work of art did not belong to him and him alone. My own Will was, perhaps, paying more attention to me now. And what about copies 'I', 'L' and 'M'? I continued. They had also been produced—which in Blake's case means printed, coloured, inked, sewn, etc, the whole process from start to finish, with the only exception of making the paper—solely, by Catherine, whom he called his 'shadow of delight'.

'You are my shadow of delight,' my Will said, rather appropriately; for he only saw me in my room in my shared house, in darkness, curtains drawn. I had never seen the flat he had bought by the river with his fiancée. She worked as a literary agent in London, made a lot of money. I told him he could do what he wanted, so he turned me over and made love to me from behind while he caressed me down there; and I came twice and he was happy.

Mrs Blake's White

Printing is a messy business. I can mostly operate my Columbian Press on my own; but it is much better if somebody else acts as the 'clean hands' while I do the inkling and the messy bits. Blake owned a rolling press. This kind of press is a thing to behold—there is a replica at Rice University that you can look at online if you are interested. Massive force needs to be applied to the rolling wheel for the printing to happen satisfactorily. You need to be strong, to believe in what you are doing, not to doubt for a second; you need to turn the wheel with decision. Very square, upright, it also looks remarkably like a miniature guillotine, or some other torture device. Or perhaps I possess a devious mind ...

Where does authorship rest? Are these exclusively Blake's artworks, or is it a tad more nuanced? Perhaps the question is about process: how close a collaborator was Catherine if she could print, entirely by herself, posthumous copies of her husband's works? How deeply involved was she in the creative process itself that produced these objects? A quick internet search reveals that her involvement was in fact tremendous. Catherine manufactured the colours, mixed them, applied them, gained enough mastery on the way for one of these colours to become known as 'Mrs Blake's White'. I thought that would be a great title for my dissertation.

Catherine operated the rolling press herself when needed. She acted as 'clean hands' on occasion. She helped maintaining the copper-plates—these too are fragile, and presumably needed to be recalibrated, maybe even re-done, after a certain number of uses. She also becomes the one thing Blake most needs: a believer. Catherine married Blake at nineteen, signing the 1782 marriage register at Battersea Church with an 'X'. William teaches her to read. William teaches her to write. William teaches her to draw. William teaches her to operate his rolling press. William teaches her to colour his prints, both applying ink and water-colouring covers, two different, equally essential processes for the final images that have come to us. And, as soon as he meets her, he confides about the 'bright angelic wings' in Peckham, seen as a boy. No disbelief from her, if we are to credit the sources, but blind, pure faith: in him, in his prophetic visions. The next thing William teaches Catherine to do is *to have visions*.

Blake's printing process was unique: it had been revealed to him by the ghost/angel of his brother Robert at the time of Robert's dying. It is understandable that the control of this process falls to him. So he moulded her, from an early age, to assist him. But Catherine grows into her role, becomes a collaborator, shares the entirety of the press's work. Not simply a colourist, not simply an apprentice. Printing, enabling, completing his vision. With the passing of years she became other needed things, filled other needed roles, as women tend to do: his curator, his accountant, his business partner. Why, then, a life as an angelic shadow? Why, then, woman as maker, never a creator? Why, then, woman as worker-bee, never as equal?

And what of love, you may ask? Love is the rolling press, love is the copperplates. Love is the operation of the machine for *America*, for *Europe*, for *Jerusalem*, for countless others; love is the operation of the machine for the *Songs*! Love is in the printing and the engraving, in creating the colours, in colouring the water-coloured covers. Like the cover of copy 'A' of *Europe*, the colouring so sublime, the subtlety of the traces...

They are both visionaries. They are both seers. But who moulds whom? Women don't control the collections, the access. Women don't control their own bodies, their marriages, their partnerships. When it was clear she would not conceive a child, William tries to introduce another woman into their domestic arrangements.

My Will makes a revelation: Jen is having miscarriage after miscarriage. He is thinking about leaving her. He doesn't say he is thinking about leaving her for me. But the implication is clear. I am fifteen years younger than Jen. I know, for I have internet-stalked her often.

She is picture-perfect, that kind of blonde, London professional with perfect hair and expensive-looking dresses; all my dresses come from the charity shops in Burleigh Street. I wonder what Will sees when he looks at me. A younger body? A fertile body? Later on, when we are at it, and he is saying 'Kate, oh Kate,' he also says that he will marry me instead; but I am not sure he means it. He is far too excited, would say anything. He also says that he will marry me instead, so therefore I won't have to write my dissertation. There will be no need for me to study any more. Am I not happy now?

Shadow Women / Invisible Wives

Catherine's belief in him was so absolute that she abandoned herself to the believing. This disappearing, this melting, suits Blake: he thought that a woman, a companion, was what he called an 'emanation': formed from man, both animated by one soul, two halves that should not be parted, with the man in the lead. On his deathbed, he muttered to her: 'You have ever been an angel to me'.

Women who dissolve into their partner's visions, in their careers. Women who dissolve into their husband's world, women who stop existing, women who vanish, women who become invisible. *Oh, my shadow of delight!* Woman not as a real thing, but as a second half, bounded by fate to her master. Angelical, ethereal beings. This is dangerous, so dangerous. For we are all in danger of vanishing, of disappearing, of melting. I have my first vision one night, after Will has left. I am alone in my room, missing him. I know I should not miss him, I know this is a slippery slope. He hasn't mentioned leaving her again.

EUROPE, A PROPHECY, COPY 'A', C. 1795, YALE CENTER FOR BRITISH ART, YALE UNIVERSITY

Fast-forward, and I am at the Yale Center for British Art, admiring copy 'A' of *Europe a Prophecy*. Printed in 1794-5, not a posthumous copy; it is, however, one whose cover has been identified as completely coloured-in by Catherine Blake, hence my trip here.

It is delicate and sorrowful and the most beautiful thing I have ever beheld. I long to touch it; I know I may not touch it. A million dollar art-work, a million dollar book of poems, lovingly produced by two geniuses.

Will married Jen last summer, and I went through despair. Had to leave my job in the library, for he was being awful: he married her, but decided that everything had been my fault somehow, punished me at work mercilessly.

I started having visions, of Catherine Blake surrounded by angels, operating the rolling press, beautifully colouring covers on her own, like the one I had come to see. But before the visions came the dreams. The first time Will had kissed me we were in my shed. He'd heard I had inherited a printing press, and said he wanted to see it. Once we were there, he came behind me, turned me to face him, and we kissed. I had wanted to, I know that. Shortly after his wedding, I started to dream of meeting him in the shed again, next to the press, of making love to him on top of it. This would be impossible, uncomfortable, and stupid. The visions were nicer than the dream. I would be in bed, but awake, and the ceiling would open up, and I would see heaven; and there, surrounded by angels, Catherine Blake operating her husband's rolling press.

My GP said I was having a mental breakdown, of all things. But I felt fine, absolutely fine. She put me on medication, and I got better. I don't have visions any more.

The AHRC grant saved me, just in time: I am writing my thesis about Catherine Blake. It is a really good topic for me, it unites all my interests; I could, I hope, write something really good about this. If only, if only ... Can I really do it? Will laughed the last time I saw him, when I explained this was happening. 'You'll never hack it,' he said. He is still angry at me. I myself am not sure of what I have done to make him so. Perhaps wanting to write my dissertation.

As I look upon it, the light shines from above, and the clouds open within the gallery. An angel, a winged, ethereal being, smiles at me from above. I see Catherine again; I knew she would never desert me.

All is well in the world.

Acknowledgements

In September 2023 I attended the Chartered Institute of Library and Information Professionals Rare Books and Special Collections Group Conference. It was entitled 'Old Hands: New Ideas', and it dealt mainly with the use of Generative AI technology in library collections. AIs have been used in major heritage collections for years now; some of the Generative AI that I use in 'Player/Creator/Emissary' is imagined, and some already exists. For example, X-Ray Microtomography, used to help us see into sealed objects, or else Transkribus, whose name I have borrowed for my story. And there are others equally terrifying. The moral dilemma inherent to the story, how to decide which generated metadata or enhanced metadata could be allowed within our collections, is a question that heritage professionals are already asking themselves.

My friend Vida Cruz-Borja provided me with the names of many of the delicious fruits depicted in 'Pink-Footed'. I will forever be grateful to her for this and other forms of support and friendship. I am equally thankful to all my other Clarion friends: this is a story that I first workshopped in San Diego a decade ago. Special thanks go to Ann VanderMeer, who told me to stop writing for my cats.

My Norwegian translator, Kathleen Rani Hagen, commissioned me to write the piece around which I wrote 'The Iceberg in my Living Room'. The aim was to publish it as a part of the Norwegian Writer's Climate Campaign. Sadly, with a newborn in tow, I never delivered it. I am therefore paying a debt. The story is dedicated to her for that reason, with apologies for the many years of delay.

'Fox & Raven' has connections to another one of my stories, 'The Ravisher, The Thief'. It is meant to imagine the years anteceding the apocalyptic world of that story.

I live in the East of England, and 'Voyage to the White Sea' stems from my interest in Anglo-Saxon culture. It has been losely inspired by Ohthere's journey into the Arctic, which he narrated to King Alfred. I have reimagined the exploit, and I beg forgiveness for mutating Alfred into a Queen: after all, Anglo-Saxon Queens existed in East Anglia. Why not remember them?

The stories in 'What Would Kate Bush Do?' are all real. They come from news reports, and transmitted female knowledge. I find a lot of solace in Kate Bush's music. I also believe that women need to be exposed early on to empowering forms of female narrative and creativity. Bush's songs contain all the answers: I've only scraped the surface of their power.

I beg forgiveness for the couple of stories that 'resemble', rather than being, poems. I can only say that I understand short-story writing as a space for experimentation, exploration, having fun, and thank readers for their patience.

I also am indebted to the editors who have allowed me to experiment during the years, in particular the ones who published earlier or finalised versions of these stories: Tim Jarvis, Dan Coxon, Sofía Rhei, Aki Schilz, Kit Caless, Lyz Grzyb and Cat Sparks.

My 'Team-Alex' writer friends give me all kinds of encouragement, companionship, and advice on a daily basis. In the matter of this book, they also saved me from myself. Thank you. Huge thanks also to all admired writers who read and endorsed this book: you're all an endless source of inspiration.

Thanks to Anita Elizabeth and Oliver Julius for their love and encouragement. This book, like all the others, is for you both. Also, thanks to James, who agreed to publish it in a list comprising far superior poetry and translated works: I am forever grateful to have sneaked in there.

At the end of each book I tend to thank the musicians I have most obsessively listened to while writing; I thought this time I would offer a closer idea of what I've been listening to in the form of the short playlist below.

Lastly, one topic that became all-encompassing as I put this collection together was what to do with intrusive forms of generative AI. The stories in this book, with all their faults and problems, have been written in their entirety by my human mind and heart. It is possible to ask any of these generation engines to write a story 'in the style of Marian Womack'. If you do this, and venture into the literary and metaphorical horrors of AI—understanding that these creatures are trained by cannibalising not only my work, but that of many others, in a Frankenstein patchwork of voices—the results should illustrate one thing: that we cannot allow our creativity to be taken over by such devices. Let's train them to do our dishes instead.

MARIAN WOMACK
Cambridge, July 2024

Bonus Track
Out Of The Window, Into The Dark Mini-Playlist:

Oh to Be in Love	*Kate Bush*
Peut-être	*Keren Ann*
Child Boy	*Lanimal*
Hold	*Flora Hibberd*
Estoy bien	*Gata Cattana*
Go Long	*Joanna Newsom*
Ma jeunesse fout le camp	*Françoise Hardy*
Whisht, the Wild Workings of the Mind	
	Lisa O'Neill
Portrait of a Dead Girl	*The Last Dinner Party*
I Know the End	*Phoebe Bridgers*

This edition of
Out of the Window, Into the Dark
was sent to print
on 18 August 2024,
anniversary of the 1812 Lady Ludd Riots,
Luddite actions carried out
by women and boys in Leeds

C

CALQUE PRESS